The Raven's
Flesh and Bones

The Raven's Flesh and Bones

Book One

Amanda Lane and **Jessica Swanborg**

Ravenmarked Sisters Publishing

This book is a work of fiction. Names, characters, places, and incidents either are products of the authors' imagination or are used fictitiously. Any resemblance to actual events or locales or persons, living or dead, is entirely coincidental.

Copyright © 2025 by Amanda Lane and Jessica Swanborg
All rights reserved.

Cover art copyright © 2025 by Jessica Swanborg
Illustrations and maps © 2025 by Jessica Swanborg

First edition, 2025
Published by
Ravenmarked Sisters Publishing

ravenmarkedsisters@theravensfleshandbones.com
www.theravensfleshandbones.com

ISBN 978-1-0696893-0-6 (pbk)
ISBN 978-1-0696893-3-7 (hc)
ISBN 978-1-0696893-1-3 (ebook)
ISBN 978-1-0696893-2-0 (audio)

10 9 8 7 6 5 4 3 2 1

Acknowledgments

We would like to extend our gratitude to all our beta readers, Nicole Miranda, Tricia Davidson, Jennifer Kwasnycia, Sereaha Burton, and Malik Aikman for taking the time to read through our story and help us to polish this world.

Thank you to all our people, who we held verbally hostage over the past year, and our families for the support and for not complaining (much) about the countless hours we had to spend on the phone together to bring this story to life.

Jessica, I never would have finished this book without your guidance and gorgeous brain. Thank you for jumping into this world headfirst with me. I am forever grateful for you.

Amanda, I can't thank you enough for pulling me into this project and allowing me to throw my crazy ideas at you, pretty much 24/7. I'm so proud of this world we have created together.

Dedication

To my beautiful boys, Elijah and Xander, and my husband Devonte for cheering me on and pushing me to keep going no matter what.

-Amanda

For my biggest cheerleaders, my babies, Silas and Abel, and my husband Anthony. And for Grandpa and Grandma for the hands you had in raising me and shaping the person behind the storytelling.

-Jessica

Content Warning

This book explores dark fantasy and supernatural themes. It contains material that some readers may find upsetting, including but not limited to, strong language, graphic violence, domestic violence, body horror, death, and child loss.
Reader discretion is strongly advised.

PART ONE

Chapter One

    The Forest is too quiet. Too still. The kind of silence that comes just before something awful.
    Alara moves through it like a shadow, her boots silent against the mossy ground, dagger in hand. The blade's green runes glow faintly in the dark, casting soft light over claw-scarred trees and churned up dirt. The scent of sweet decay lingers in the air.
    They'd been coming for days now, twisting through the trees at night. Ripping apart livestock, ravaging fields of grain, and two children. Gone. Disappeared without a trace.
    She scans the ground beneath her. Intestines, blood, and half-chewed organs decorate the forest floor. She prays it's from the goats.

The village whispers her name in times like these.
Alara.
Hunter. Killer. Protector.
She doesn't care what they call her. She cares that monsters are threatening their home. Taking from it. Tearing it apart.
A twig snaps.
She freezes.
She hears the clicking of the teeth. The sound grows louder, slipping beneath her skin.
Here we go.
It lunges from the fog. A creature with four long limbs and black skin that's stretched too tight over bones, like wax over sticks. Its jaw opens unnaturally wide, skinny teeth like needles clacking in rows.
She plunges the dagger into its gut, twisting as the green light flares. The creature shrieks, high and short. It crumples to the ground. It didn't stand a chance.
One.
She hears the clicking to her left. She spins fast—
Too slow.
Razor sharp claws rake across her shoulder, ripping through leather and flesh. She cries out and stumbles forward, her breath catching in her throat as the creature's poison enters her blood.
NeedleTeeth.

This one larger than the last, chittering madly as it crawls slowly around her. Daring her to make a move.

Alara exhales and lunges at it, sliding under the creature. She slices its belly wide open with her blade. Blood and innards spill out, pouring over her. A shower from hell.

Two.

Her arm throbs, searing hot from the venom. Her own blood drips beneath her sleeve. She wipes her face with her coat, rubbing the monster's gore from her eyes.

A third one wriggles down from the trees, crawling low on seemingly broken limbs. Its teeth click like a stone filled rattle.

Alara stands there, humming as it circles her. A soft melody. An old lullaby.

The NeedleTeeth creeps closer, its tongue writhing at the smell of her blood.

She leaps at it, sinking the steel into its spine. A flash of green shines from the runes her mother had once etched by hand. The creature collapses, twitching at her feet.

Three.

She keeps humming. Drawing the nightmares that lurk in the dark. Baiting them.

The fourth comes crashing down on her from the treetops, no sound this time, just weight, slamming her into the forest floor. Claws tear the earth beneath her, jaws thrashing violently towards her throat. The creature's skin is wrong.

Rubbery and wet, like stretched leather left too long in the rain. Bones press back against its skin, jutting unnaturally beneath its surface, as though it had been sewn together by madness. Its jaws snap inches from her face now—*clickclickclick*—tiny needle like teeth chittering as they fight to sink into her flesh.

Alara grits her teeth and shoves her forearm into its neck to hold it back. Hot drool spills onto her chest, burning her skin like acid. A small whimper escapes her lips. Its claws dig at the dirt beside her head, inches from tearing open her skull.

Too close. Too heavy. Too fast.

Alara's dagger falls from her grasp. It lays in the moss, just out of reach.

She jerks her body sideways, twisting beneath the beast, screaming as its sharp elbow drives into the gash on her shoulder. Her arm remains on the NeedleTeeth's neck, pushing it back as she cries out with blinding pain. With a snarl she grabs a fist full of its flesh and twists, peeling it back from its bones. It screeches and falters momentarily, long enough for her fingers to brush the steel.

She closes her hand around the hilt and thrusts it upwards under its jaw. The green runes ignite like fire.

The creature spasms violently. It shrieks, one long warbling scream, before slumping over.

Four.

Alara lies panting beneath its weight, chest heaving, every muscle aching. She's soaked in blood and acid. Her ribs throb and her hands shake.

But she is alive. And it is not.

Alara pushes the creature off her. It thumps to the ground. She stumbles to her feet, breathing heavily. There's blood on her face, her clothes, her hands. The dagger hisses as the magic cools and the blood burns off.

She hears a sharp breath from the shadows behind her. She whips around, ready for another attack.

From a nearby brush, she spots a pair of eyes—blue, wide. Full of awe and fear. "Alec..." she breathes.

Her little brother, curled up in the underbrush like a guilty fox, twigs in his golden curls, lips parted in shock. Alec raises his hand to his mouth. He wears his leather-braided bracelet, the bronze catching the moonlight. The protection sigil Alara had carved there forks out, chiselled into the metal like a promise.

"You followed me?"

"I just wanted to see," he whispers, "how you do it..."

She walks towards him, fury and pain pounding in rhythm. "I told you to stay in the cottage, Alec."

5

"I know but—" He glances at the bodies of the beasts she had just put down. "You were singing that song... The one... mama used to sing."

Her rage flickers, turning into something raw. Grief. Memory...

He looks up at her. "I liked it," he says quietly. "And I saw how good you are..."

"What you saw was me almost becoming NeedleTeeth food," she growls at him.

Disappointment flashes across his face. Tears well up behind his big blue eyes. She sighs and drops to crouch beside him, wincing at the pain shooting through her body. "You're lucky one of them didn't hear you instead of me."

"I stayed hidden really good! Just like you taught me," his voice chimes with small pride.

She looks him over. No blood. Not a scratch. Just big wide eyes and too much trust in his sister.

"You can never do this again," she scolds, pulling him to his feet and out of the bush.

"I won't, I promise." He looks up at her with awe and worry. "That was really scary," he says, "but you weren't afraid."

She lets out a breath, almost a chuckle. "Alec, I'm always afraid." Alara holds her hand out for him. He takes it. "Come on, let's get home."

Alec walks beside her in silence for a while, his short legs working hard to keep up. "You're kind of terrifying," he says finally.

She smiles. "Good."

By the time they reach their cottage, Alara's legs are barely holding her up. Blood soaks through her coat, the leather stiff and tacky from the drying gore. Alec has gone quiet. He has seen far too much for any eight-year-old to bear. Alara suspects the horrors from tonight will soon find him in his nightmares.

She shoves open the wooden door with her uninjured shoulder, almost falling over the threshold. She catches herself on the door frame and motions for Alec to go inside.

The familiar scent of dried herbs and soot greets them. A fire Alec had forgotten to put out has died, leaving orange and red embers behind. Alara will scold him for that another night. Alec drops onto his small cot in the corner, curling his legs underneath him.

She moves past him, towards the washbasin. Her hands tremble as she removes her bloodied coat, then the tunic beneath, gritting her teeth as the fabric clings to her wounds. She peels it away from the jagged tear in her shoulder, slowly, humming to herself through the sharp pain. The gash is angry and raw. The veins surrounding it black with the NeedleTeeth's poison. She grabs a cloth and the jug of water she leaves beside the washbasin for such an occasion, pouring it over the cloth. She dabs the edges, hissing as the cold touches the fire-hot pain.

"You're bleeding a lot," Alec murmurs.

"Thanks," she says through clenched teeth, "but it's not all mine." She winks at him to let him know she's alright.

"Your chest looks... messed up."

She glances down. A blotchy red burn spreads from her collarbone to her breastbone where the creature's acidic drool had soaked through. She blots at it, the cloth sticking to the wound.

Alara tosses the cloth aside and reaches for a small, pale-green jar of healing salve. Her mother had taught her how to make it—comfrey, blood moss, witch hazel, and a small incantation to activate it. It stings something fierce but it works well.

She spreads the balm over the gash and acid-scorched skin with steady fingers, through her swimming vision.

Alec still watches her. He's quiet for a moment.

"Why do you do it?" he finally asks.

"Because it has to be done," she smiles at him sweetly. "Do you expect old farmer Jerrick to hunt?" She chuckles at the thought of him hobbling into the woods with his cane.

"But why do you go after them *alone?*" He asks sheepishly.

She doesn't look up, scrubbing fiercely at the blood that drenches her. "I didn't know what I was dealing with yet. I couldn't trust that whoever I brought with me would come back."

"Does it hurt?"

She meets his eyes, "Every time."

There are no more questions, no more talk, as Alec's breathing grows heavier and sleep consumes him. Alara finishes cleaning the blood from her skin. She wraps her shoulder, now caked in salve and quietly steps to the corner where Alec lies, sound asleep. She runs her fingers through his curls and places a gentle kiss on his forehead, before turning into her own bed. She drags her ratty old blanket over her body and listens to Alec's deep steady breathing. She may get a couple hours of sleep tonight, if the adrenaline can settle.

Chapter Two

I sit in the grass, the heat from the sun warming my legs. The sky is clear and baby blue, a stark contrast to the usual cloud-covered grey. Birds are singing in nearby trees where they've built their homes and tend to their young. I can hear water lapping against earth somewhere in the distance.

Alec sits across from me, barefoot and grinning, a little dirt on his cheek. He looks younger than he should.

Four? Maybe five?

He watches my hands as I draw a symbol in the dirt with my index finger.

"Now," I say softly, "trace it exactly. And feel the pull, not just the shape."

He nods, tongue poking out from the corner of his mouth in concentration as he mimics my movements.

A protection key. The first sigil our mother ever taught me.

There's joy here. It's quiet. The kind of peace I forgot existed.

He looks up at me with his big curious eyes. "Like this?"

"Perfect," I say, smiling. "You're getting good."

Clickclickclickclickclick

I jump at the sound in the distance. It splits the air around us. I freeze. Alec does too.

The sky darkens. The sun doesn't set—it dies, smothered to death by shadows.

Something rises from the earth behind Alec. No face. No eyes. Just antlers and bone. Its robes are made of smoke and ruin. The smell of metal and decay follows it from beneath.

"Run," I whisper.

But he doesn't. He doesn't move.

"Alec, run!" I shout, urging him to get up.

He remains still. I grab his hands, trying to pull him to his feet. He doesn't budge, as if his body is fused to the grass and dirt beneath him.

"Alara..." his voice is weak and breaks halfway through my name. He looks at me with wide eyes but his normal curious stare has been replaced with a fear I have never seen. His skin begins to flake all shades of grey. His fingers go

11

quick, crumbling into the breeze. "What's happ—" His face blows in the wind.

"No!" I scream as I lunge for him, trying to grab up his little body. My hands pass through him, tightening around his shoulders as they shatter and drift away. I reach for his waist, pulling him into me but that too turns to ash, disintegrating from my touch, like a log that had been on fire far too long. I scream his name as I grab at his ashes in handfuls, as if I can put him back together. I sink to my knees, my hands cupping his remains. His curls, his skin, his laugh, all reduced to soot in my palms.

I can't breathe.

It's still there... The shadow. Its silhouette is a mountain glowering down at me with absent eyes.

It speaks to me, its voice echoing in my head, slithering at the back of my skull. The space is silent but *I* can hear it. The sound of a thousand whispers breathing as one, old and wet. *The blood is mine,* it hisses.

There's no sky now. Only smoke and bones, antlers and ashes. Stretching, expanding. Taking over.

I try to move but the ground becomes like quicksand. Heavy and pulling me down. Ash becomes mud. Mud becomes blood. Blood becomes hands. Hands rooted together in a demonic dance. Clawing, grabbing at me, sinking its bony fingers into my skin. I try to fight, to no avail. They pull me down beneath the surface. Thick, hot, metallic blood fills my mouth, choking me to death.

The blood is mine.

Alara shoots up in her bed, coughing and gasping for air like she's just surfaced from deep, thick water. Sweat slicks her skin. Her chest rises and falls in sharp jerks.

Feathers float in the air around her, drifting in slow spirals as gravity pushes them down. Her pillow is in ruins. She has torn it open in her sleep again. Down clings to her hair, her night gown, her sticky skin.

From the other side of the room Alec stirs. "Did you fight your pillow again?" he asks groggily.

"Apparently," she sighs as she plucks a feather from her auburn locks. "Looks like I won." She looks to Alec, hoping to get a giggle. He doesn't respond. It's been said one too many times.

Alec sits up, just enough to inspect the carnage. "That's the third one this month. You're going to have to ask Deia to make you another one."

Alara exhales deeply. "I'll add it to the list. Right after killing monsters and making sure you don't sneak out again."

He grins, seemingly unbothered.

Rising from her bed, she walks over to the washbasin and splashes her face with cold water.

The chill is sharp and cleansing but it makes her want to crawl back under her covers. She pauses in front of the cracked mirror hanging off-kilter from the wall. It catches her reflection in pieces, scattering her, splitting her in five crooked directions. Green stormy eyes stare back through the slivers of glass. Her dark hair shines red as the sun peaks through the tattered curtains, catching it. It spills wildly over her shoulders, still damp. Feathers are tucked into the loose strands like some kind of cursed halo. Her fingers drift to the necklace resting against her collar bone—a small sun spiral, carved from brass and darkened with age. The elders had gifted it to her after her mother's passing. A custom older than the village itself. A way to keep the dead tethered to the living. Her thumb lingers on the curve of the spiral, tracing its edges.

  She barely remembers the ceremony but she remembers the cold hands that fastened the pendant around her neck. With a slow breath, she lets it fall back into place. She plucks the feathers from her hair and ties it back in its usual low knot.

  Her shoulder pulls sharply as she rotates her arm, gauging the damage from the night before. She peels away the linen wrap and inspects the wound. The gash has closed more than halfway, the veins surrounding it now a less threatening crimson. The burns along her collarbone and chest have faded to a pale pink with little protrusion.

She dips two fingers into the jar of salve sitting on the shelf beside the mirror and spreads it gently over the damaged skin. It doesn't sting this time, just tingles. A cold sensation rushes over the half-open skin on her shoulder.

Alec leans back on his elbows. "Still going to the council meeting?"

Alara nods, not turning from the mirror. "I shouldn't be long."

"They're going to be mad at you," Alec teases.

"Let them," she responds. "I killed four NeedleTeeth last night. That's more than the other hunters would have done in." She smiles to herself proudly.

She slips her boots on and reaches for her coat, remembering that it needs a good wash in the creek. Instead of wearing it, she drapes the stiff leather over her arm, adding it to her list for the day. Her dagger lies on the small wooden table beside her bed. She straps it to her thigh.

At the threshold she pauses. "You'll stay here?" she asks over her shoulder.

"Don't leave the fence line, inside before sundown," he answers, rolling his eyes at the same old rules.

She gives him the look she always does. The kind of look a mother gives their naughty child. "And no following me."

He raises his hands in surrender. "I promise."

Alara steps out into the morning light. A small cold breeze tugs at her hair. She peers out at the shredded fields of barley and wheat. Just beyond the fence line she catches something moving, frozen in place, yet swaying gently.
Lily.
She is pale as ever. Her blotchy, yellow skin rots on her face, the right side mangled, leaving her jawbone exposed. She moves slowly in place—stuck, sunken into the overgrown grass and brambles, as if she'd sprouted amongst them many years ago. One of her eyes is clouded white, the other nearly hidden beneath a heavy, drooping lid, giving her an eerie, lopsided gaze. She makes a low, raspy wheeze as she rocks, trying to free herself from the bushes.
Later.
Alara makes a mental note to deal with Lily after the council meeting. Freeing the undead from brambles isn't exactly urgent, though it is disturbingly routine.

The sun is climbing as Alara reaches the village square, though its warmth barely cuts through the crisp morning air. She keeps her head down as she walks but eyes follow her all the same. They always do.

The old Chapel looms at the end of the square, its foundation cracked, the stained-glass windows long since shattered and replaced with plain panes. Engravings of old Gods no one prays to anymore still stand tall in the stone, waiting. The wooden doors groan open as she steps inside. The noise hits her like a wave. Dozens of villagers fill the main chamber. The wooden pews creak under the weight of too many bodies and too much panic. Voices overlap in a mess of worry and terror.

"They shredded the barley fields! What's left won't feed us through the first frost!"
"They took the livestock! Tore it to bits!"
"Two children! Two!"
"What are we supposed to eat?"
"Scratches on the roof!
"The roof!"

Alara stands in the doorway. The once sacred hall stretches before her, high-vaulted and hollow. The old altar has been repurposed into a table for the lead council members. Its carvings weathered but readable. Gods erased but not gone.

Someone notices her.

"Alara."

Like a spell, her name ripples through the crowd. One by one, yet all at once, the villagers fall silent, turning to face her.

She walks down the center aisle, her boots thudding heavy against the stone floor.

The council leaders sit at the old altar on a platform in front of the villagers. Seated in chairs carved in old style, faded and mismatched. In the center, hunched in the largest seat, sits elder Tilda.

Her bones are as thin as her mouth. Her beady eyes follow Alara like a hawk.

Beside her sits two of her trusted advisors. Councilman Thomas on her right, a permanent scowl pulling at his features. His white hair is combed carefully over the thinning patch atop his head. His finger taps impatiently against the wooden table.

Councilwoman Elowen sits on the right, her hood drawn low, shadows veiling half her face. Her hands are folded in her lap as she watches on in silence.

The village's three appointed hunters stand beside the table.

Bram, with shoulders wide enough to carry a cow but a voice too soft to carry anger. His dark hair falls messily against his forehead. He tilts his head slightly as she approaches, his brown eyes squinting as he examines her.

Maren, tall and angular, arms crossed. Her short blonde hair falls perfectly in place. Her sneer always arriving before her words.

And Auryn—quiet, calculating, always watching. His soft hazel eyes contrast with his dark skin and long black braids. He offers Alara a small nod—subtle but sincere. The only one of the trio that meets her with that sort of quiet kindness.

Alara stops in front of them beneath the platform, facing the council.

Elder Tilda's voice rasps through the silence. "Tell us what happened."

Alara doesn't flinch. "Four of them are dead." Whispers break out behind her.

"Were they the only ones?" someone asks—perhaps a worried mother.

"I don't know," Alara answers. "I followed their trail into the forest. It ended near Hollow Creek but I didn't find a nest. Not yet."

Another voice rises, "You went alone?"

Bram shifts but doesn't look at her. "She went without us. Again."

Alara keeps her gaze on Tilda. "There wasn't time to gather a party. And I wasn't sure what we were dealing with. I acted when I heard the sound coming through the trees."

"No." Maren's voice is shrill and annoyed. "You *chose* not to wait. You never wait."

Alara turns slowly to meet her curled up sneer. "I waited last time. And the shepherd's son didn't make it home."

A hush spreads through the room.

Maren's lips press into a thin line.

"Enough," Auryn says, taking a step forward. "Arguing about timing won't bring anyone back. We need a plan."

Tilda raises a hand, silencing the hunters. "These creatures. Describe them."

Alara nods. "I call them NeedleTeeth. Big, twisted. Wet, black skin. Rows of teeth too skinny to make sense. Like sewing needles. They make a clicking sound with their teeth. Loud enough to warn you they are near... *Usually.*"

19

Someone gags near the back of the room.
"They tear through wood like it's paper. I'm lucky I didn't lose my arm last night," she says as she turns towards the villagers and pulls back the collar of her blouse, revealing the jagged wound on her shoulder.
Silence.
"They don't eat. They destroy."
"And the children?" A woman whispers.
Alara hesitates, "I don't know."
Another voice, this one less restrained. "Will there be more?"
Alara looks out at them, at all the familiar faces, at the fear and panic they wear.
"I'm not sure," she says. "But this could be the beginning. I need to push further. There were some signs of tunnels. If there's a nest, I'll find it."
Bram steps forward now, "*We* will find it."
Maren lifts her chin, her face still wearing her disdain as she looks down her skinny nose at Alara. "If we're not too slow."
Alara stares back at her. "You'll slow me down if you don't listen."
"We *will* listen," Auryn says with a steady voice. "You'll need us if you find the nest and we want to help." He nods at her again. A silent alliance.
Alara returns the gesture. "We leave tonight."

20

Tilda leans forward, her chair creaking as she moves. "Find their nest. Find the children. End this," she commands.

Chapter Three

    Alara kneels at the creek's edge, sleeves rolled up, her coat bundled in her hands. The leather is stiff with dried blood and viscera. She scrubs in firm, practiced circles, watching the red and brown colours swirl away downstream as she keeps her hands working. Her shoulder aches with each motion.
    The forest around her is quiet. Not safe—never safe. But still, for the moment. Her humming echoes off the stone, the dirt walls amplifying the steady notes.
    She likes this spot. Tucked behind a curtain of reeds and low branches. She would often come here when her skin felt too tight. When she couldn't silence her thoughts. Or the stares and

whispers from the village started to get to her. She would dip her feet into the cold water, enjoying the pull of the stream. She would come here when she craved the silence.

She hears a soft rustling from the other side of the creek. She doesn't look up right away. She stops rubbing at her coat, shaking her head slowly at the creature on the other side. When she finally lifts her gaze, she finds exactly what she is expecting.

A Scab.

It stands, half-slouched over a leaning birch tree. Its limbs are long and thin, like a sloppy scarecrow. Someone has taken the time to dress it. The fabric is damp, barely covering the yellow, blotchy skin between its legs. It has the same stupid look on its face that they always do, accompanied by those familiar, milky eyes.

"Not today," she mutters.

It twitches and stares vacantly, its jaw hanging wide open.

Alara picks up a smooth stone, running her finger over the surface for a moment, a sort of grounding against the chaos of the day. She aims and chucks it into the creek. Water splashes up like an explosion, droplets shooting towards its half-decayed body, hitting its legs and torso.

The Scab jolts and lets out a low, airy grunt before hobbling off into the trees in a stumbled half-jog.

Alara rolls her eyes, "Get your own stream."

She doesn't turn when she hears the crunching of boots behind her. "I could hear you stomping from the trees," she says dryly. "Not very stealthy of you."

Bram gives a tired chuckle, "We weren't trying to sneak. Auryn thought you might be here."

"I figured she'd be brooding somewhere dramatic," Maren mutters, "didn't think it'd be laundry day."

Alara wrings out one of the sleeves of her coat and looks over her shoulder. "Nice to see your witty charm made it out of the chapel intact."

Auryn gives her a faint smirk as he sits on a nearby stone, draping his arms over his knees. "Maren's always charming," he laughs.

"Let me guess," Alara says, slinging her damp coat over a slab of stone. "You came to complain?"

Bram sits on the other side of Alara, pulling off his boots and socks. He plunges his feet into the rushing stream. "We came to talk." He throws his head back with closed eyes and takes a deep breath through his nostrils. "You know, I used to come out here for some peace," he smiles. A small longing smile, just for a second, before his face drops. "That was before my mother got sick." The bags under his eyes have grown larger. His mother has been fading for months now. When he's not tracking monsters, he's by her side, holding a hand that doesn't squeeze back.

"Wow, this is the most emotion I think I've ever seen from you, Bram," Alara jokes, slipping back into her usual mental armour.

"It happens on occasion." He meets her eyes for a fleeting moment, just long enough for Alara to see the pain behind them.

"I'm sorry, should we have brought some ale for this pity party?" Maren interjects, clearly annoyed. Alara doesn't need to look at her to know she is still wearing her usual contorted face.

"That would've made it easier to deal with you," Alara bites back. She throws a sly grin in Maren's direction, snapping her fingers ironically. "Next time."

Bram raises a hand, keeping the peace. "Like I said, we're here to talk."

"About what our next move is," Auryn adds.

"And to make sure you don't run off again." Maren's voice grows more aggravating by the second.

Alara scoffs loudly. "How else would I get away from you?"

"Come on, girls," Bram warns. "This isn't why we're here. We only have a few hours of sun. What's the plan?"

Maren kicks at the dirt under her boot, carving an annoying hole in Alara's quiet place. "It's obvious, isn't it? We find the nest and burn them out," she states with confidence.

Alara stands to face her. "No."

"Why not?" Maren crosses her arms.

"The children!" Alara yells at her.

"So?" snaps Maren. "You think those things took them for story time?"

"No," Alara says, her voice like thunder. "But I'm not lighting a match until I know there aren't still living bodies in there." Maren stares at her, arms crossed, all sneer. "Got it?"

They glare at each other, challenging one another. Maren stands a head taller than Alara but they both know where the power lies. "Fine," Maren huffs.

Bram rubs the back of his neck. "Then what should we do?" he asks, cutting through the tension.

Alara turns back towards Bram and Auryn, blocking Maren with her shoulder. "Like I said at the meeting, I tracked them to the edge of Hollow Creek. I saw a dip there that I haven't seen before. Right before I got attacked last night."

"Tunnels, right?" Bram confirms.

"Yes, that's what I was thinking. But I didn't have time to investigate further."

Maren takes a few steps to the right, trying hard to include herself in the debriefing. "Well, that's a shame. Guess you're not as good as you think you are."

Alara's glare shoots daggers at her. "I'm ten times better than you on your best day." Maren drops her head slightly. Alara rolls her eyes and continues with the plan. "I need to head back to Ravenforge. Let Alec know I'll be out tonight. I'll

26

set up sigils around the fence to ward off the NeedleTeeth, in case they decide to return to the village while we are gone."

"Sigils?" Maren snorts.

"Yes. Sigils."

"That won't stop them from entering," Bram comments as he pulls his feet from the river and stands. Auryn follows in suit.

"No. But it will melt their faces off if they cross the barrier," Alara says, "and that will give Ravenforge time to barricade in the chapel while they wait for us to return."

Bram nods in understanding, "Okay, what's next?"

"We head to Hollow Creek, hopefully before nightfall. That'll give us the upper hand." She looks around at her fellow hunters. None of them friends by definition but the closest she's got. "Then we find a way in."

The group starts the trek back to Ravenforge in silence, apart from the occasional disapproving sigh Maren makes to let the other hunters know she's still there.

They are close enough to see the edge of the fence through the trees when they hear it. Alara's skin breaks out in raised bumps at the sound.

Clickclickclickclick.

Chapter Four

All four hunters turn to face it. It crawls unnaturally towards them, every leg out of sync, as if it were a fawn learning to walk on too long of limbs. It's slower than the others she has faced thus far. Teeth as unsettling as Alara remembers, chittering at them. But this one is different. Its body shimmers with transparent hues, flickering otherworldly.

"Fan out!" Alara commands. "Surround it! Don't let it get to the village!"

They scatter, Bram and Maren to the left, facing it as it watches them. It clicks thrice before it notices Auryn closing in from the right.

It locks eyes with Alara next. She knew it would target her. The smallest of the group. The creature leaps forward, locked and aimed. She braces for impact, drawing her dagger from her side, readying herself for the attack.

It jumps and—passes through her.

She gasps. Cold blooms in her chest like winter in her lungs. Her breath catches and her knees buckle. She nearly falls to the ground from the sensation. It scrapes through her, dragging its essence along her bones. Her stomach turns, the taste of rot churning in her belly.

The NeedleTeeth hits the ground behind her. It spins to greet her again, its claws churning up dirt as it moves. The Earth sprays around its patchwork limbs, encircling the monster in a wall of dust.

"How did you do that?" Bram shouts from behind her, confusion and shock in his voice.

"I didn't."

It wiggles at her, like a demonic cat about to pounce on its dinner.

Alara gets low and readies her weapon.

"Get back!" Maren shouts, darting in, her spear slicing wide and upwards.

"Maren!" Alara grits her teeth as Maren's move throws her off balance, forcing her to twist her body to avoid being caught between monster and steel.

The target is missed, the pike slicing through nothing but air, narrowly missing the NeedleTeeth's head. It swipes at Maren, claws making contact with her leg, shredding it to the bone. She screams in agony, falling on her side.

It goes for the kill.

Swiftly, Alara jumps at it, intercepting the blow, tackling it in another direction. Its teeth clack as it tries to shake her off its back. With lethal speed she slashes its throat from one side to the other. It makes a wet gargling sound as the blood spurts out of the mangled opening. It wobbles from side to side before collapsing.

Alara climbs down, landing on her feet with intent. She storms towards Maren, yanking her up by her shirt collar and slamming her into the nearest tree. Bark cracks and Maren lets out an unintentional grunt, one hand flying out as she tries to brace herself.

"You arrogant, reckless—"

"Get off me," Maren hisses weakly through clenched teeth.

"You almost got yourself killed! What am I to tell your father?" Maren avoids her eyes. "Did you hear me?" She shakes her roughly, trying for an explanation.

"Alara..." Auryn's voice is low and worried. Alara turns to him, still pressing Maren into the bark.

His eyes are fixed on Maren's leg. "Maybe we can do this another time. She's badly injured."

Alara follows his gaze.

Blood pools at the base of Maren's boot. Her trousers are shredded to ribbons—wet, clinging tatters, soaked in red. Her leg is flayed open from thigh to shin, the skin hanging around it. The white flash of bone glistens through the gore.

    Alara releases her from her rage-filled grip. Maren falls to the base of the tree, the weight of her own body too heavy for the moment. She clutches at the wound, breathing fast. Sweat begins to form in beads, her face losing its colour.

    "Shit," Alara mutters. She turns to Bram and Auryn. "Get her back to the village. Take her to Serilda," They share a reluctant glance but nod in agreement. "Tell her she's been poisoned. She'll know what to do."

    Bram is already moving before she can finish, crouching beside Maren, bracing her arm over his shoulder. Auryn is ready on the other side.

    Alara steps back, still seething, her fists clenched to her sides instead of around Maren's throat.

    "We've got her," Auryn huffs as they pull her upright, her injured leg dangling behind them. The three of them make their way down the path, Alara following closely behind. She reaches the fence and stops short.

    Still tangled in the brambles, hanging like a broken marionette trying to sway herself free, is Lily. Her long dress flutters faintly in the breeze, the lilies at the hem dancing in the wind. Her mottled skin splits where the vines bite into her arms and legs. Her mouth is still slack. Same as before. Stuck.

"Right," Alara exhales slowly, her anger replaced by exhaustion. "Sorry, girl," she mutters, more so to herself, as she steps off the path and makes her way towards the broken girl.

Drawing near, she spots a second figure hovering beside Lily. Her pace slows as she takes in the scene.

A boy, no older than fifteen, with matted blonde hair, stands on the other side of the fence. He holds a stone in one hand, a sharp stick in the other. "Come on, freak!" he mocks, poking the weapon through her arm. It squelches through the decay like butter. "Do something!" Lily tries to move away from the threat but she's held captive there. Panicked wheezes escape her mouldy lips.

"Hey!" Alara's voice is like a lightning strike.

The boy jumps at her sudden appearance. Without ask, he drops the stone and takes a step backwards, the stick still in his grip. The boy's shoulders are too broad for his age. She notices the golden ring around his pupils as she approaches. A young hunter.

"Is this part of your training?" She reaches over the pickets and snatches the stick from his hand.

"No, I just—"

"It's Jorin, am I right? Son of Davit?"

He nods while looking down, avoiding her eyes.

"Who is your trainer?" she asks, a sprinkle of threat in her words.

"Bram," he answers reluctantly. "He hasn't been keeping with the training, ma'am." He rubs his hands together, anxiously. "His mother has the sickness."

"You want to be a hunter?"

"Yes, ma'am," he mutters, still staring at the overgrown grass and weeds.

"Do you call this hunting?"

He doesn't respond but Alara can see the shame wash over his fragile features.

"Do you want to know what I call this?"

He meets her eyes now. She takes him in. A farmer's boy wearing ill-fitted leather, playing a cruel game. Too old to be this stupid, too young to know any better. "I call this a conversation with Bram. And your father."

"I—I'm sorry." He looks away from her again. She lets him simmer in the threat for a moment.

"I hope I've made myself clear," she says. "And if I ever catch you hurting one of them again—"

"I—I won't," he stammers. He backs away slowly, waiting to be excused before he commits.

"Go," she finally releases him.

The young hunter turns and sprints back to his home in a flash.

Alara turns towards Lily. Up close, the smell is worse. Wet. Sweet and sour, like old meat left out in the sun. Lily turns to her as she approaches. She cannot see, her clouded eyes long gone dim, though she can sense her, nonetheless. She always could.

"I didn't forget you," Alara says quietly, gently brushing the leaves from her hair. Lily twitches, a soft, husky sound escaping her lips. Alara inspects the damage caused by the boy, holding her arm tenderly. Even that feels dangerous. Her fingers ghost over Lily's wrist. She flinches at the give beneath her touch. A small oozing puncture stares at her, reminding Alara how easy it is to break this already fractured body. "I'm sorry I didn't come sooner."

Alara retrieves her dagger from her thigh, its purpose not to kill but to free. She slides the blade under the brambles, carefully, not to nick what remains of Lily's weathered skin. The vines fight against her, as if they've grown fond of the girl, as though they want to keep her. One by one she severs them, the branches shooting back to their roots with reluctant snaps.

As the last of them give way, Lily falls forward. Alara catches her in her arms. She is light, too light. Bones and decaying flesh bundled together. Lily's head drops against Alara's shoulder and for a moment they simply stand like that. An embrace between the living—and the not.

"Let's get you out of here," Alara whispers.

Lily doesn't answer. She never does.

Alara takes her hands, holding them as if they are made of wet paper. She leads her out of

34

the bush, carefully avoiding the low branches and dips, pulling her to safety.

They walk beneath the trees together for some time, Alara's fingers still tenderly wrapped around Lily's hands.

Nestled deep within the woods stands a crooked little shelter between two giant oaks. Alara had stumbled across the place years ago, back when her mother was still breathing and her world still had some semblance of peace. Lily had always been here, fragile and swaying, beside a heap of sticks bound with brittle twine, as if she were guarding a forgotten memory.

After her mother died, Alara returned to this spot. Lily was still standing beside the mess of sticks and rope. That's when Alara began to build. Not just for Lily but for them both. She packed the walls with mud and stone, hands scraped raw and heart heavier than she could handle.

The roof is a spindly lattice of those same worn sticks, lashed together with strands from the old twine that had first marked the spot as sacred. The floor is soft with time. Dried flowers lie scattered like offerings, petals curled brown but still faintly sweet, masking the sour scent that clings to Lily's skin.

It isn't beautiful but it is *theirs*. A hidden place for the girl that can't speak and the girl that chooses not to.

Alara crouches beneath the low entryway, pulling Lily gently behind her. They duck under the sagging roof. The musty scent of earth and sweet dry flowers fill her lungs—familiar, grounding. Alara guides Lily to her spot in the shelter, angling her at a lean so she doesn't slump and sits closely beside her. She props herself against the oak, feeling the hard bark press into her spine. She rests her head back and slowly exhales.

Thoughts crowd the edges of her mind but she tries to keep them at bay. Tries to keep herself from feeling the pain that threatens to creep through. For a while they sit there together. Simply existing.

"I used to imagine you were a ghost," she says finally, her voice barely a whisper. "Something to keep me company after she—" She stops, unable to bring herself to finish. There is a sudden shift in Lily's posture, as though she is trying to listen. "I don't know who you were... before *this*," she mutters, "but I hope you were loved." She reaches down and brushes a leaf from Lily's stained dress. They sit together, quietly. The silence neither awkward nor empty.

Slowly, Lily shifts. Inching herself with all the strength her feeble body can muster, until her side is pressing into Alara. Alara watches as she finds her shoulder, laying her head, resting there with a sweet softness. Alara doesn't move. She lets her stay like that, returning the gesture as she rests her own head against Lily's. A comfort they both need in the moment.

"I miss her," she murmurs. Lily doesn't reply but her hand, delicate and dirt-smudged, lifts and settles against Alara's arm, fingers curling just enough to hold on. Just enough to make Alara question how much of her is truly gone.

Scabs are said to be empty shells of the people they once were. But Lily never felt empty to Alara. She's always seemed compassionate in these moments. Always gave her a quiet sense of peace.

Inside this shoddy shelter, between two carved oaks and dead flowers, there is stillness. Understanding. Comfort. Even if it is all made up by a lonely girl grieving her mother.

Chapter Five

The sun is high as Alara exits the shelter. She blinks against it, half-expecting another cold, grey day. It is warm and light, quite odd for the season. She casts one last glance at Lily, who has resumed her usual slow sway, rocking from side to side.

"I'll come see you again," she breathes, a promise she can't hear.

The forest falls away as Alara pushes forward, trees thinning into demolished fields. Farmers trying their best to salvage and nourish what remains.

Just over three hundred souls call Ravenforge their home. Men, women, and children, all working with the purpose to keep their village thriving. Gold and coin mean very little in a place like this. Hard work and necessity stand as their currency.

    Low cottages covered in moss with soot-stained roofs stretch before her as she continues down the main footpath. Chimney smoke curls and spirals before disappearing into the sky. Children's laughter echoes through the village, vanishing as she approaches. As always. Perhaps they were told of her run-in with Jorin. Eyes and hushed whispers follow her through her journey as she passes her own home and veers off down a much narrower pathway.

    The trail is overgrown with thistle and stinging nettle. It twists through wild underbrush, begging to be cleared, to a place the villagers avoid like the plague. A little house some swear is abandoned, tucked under the outstretched limbs of a massive ash tree. Bones hang from the branches like charms, clanging in the wind.

    Alara hasn't set foot here since her mother's passing. Back then, her mother—Lyssa—would bring her and Alec for lessons, almost daily. Lyssa would set out baskets of herbs while Serilda chanted over flames. The old witch kept shelves full of journals, each one inked, filled with runes and tested incantations. Alara would study them, tracing each line until her eyes blurred. The windows still glow with a strange light that even the sun cannot snuff out.

    Alara reaches the battered door. Its edges are splintered from years of wind and wear. She knocks as a formality but enters without invitation. The door creaks eerily as she swings it open and steps inside.

    Inside the air is warm with herbs and memories. Candles burn in colours that don't belong to this world. A line of crushed petals mark the floor like a forgotten ritual.

    Auryn stands near the hearth of the fire, his arms crossed. His skin glows a deep honey colour in the odd lighting. Bram leans against the corner to her left, scraping dry blood from his coat sleeve with a dull knife. On a cot between the two, leg swaddled tight in blood-stained bandages, lies Maren. Pale, lips tight with sweat that glistens across her brow. She breathes shakily through clenched teeth.

    "You've grown," a familiar voice chimes. Alara turns to find Serilda, sitting at a small wobbly table, stirring something furiously in a large, cracked bowl. She looks barely older than Alara—tall, sharp-boned, with long, uncombed black hair. Her skin is too smooth and youthful for someone whispered to be centuries old. "Not taller, sadly. But meaner, certainly," she says, speaking to Alara, her eyes glued to her mixing bowl.

    "I'm not here for a reunion, Auntie," Alara tells her.

    "You and the boy never come to see me anymore..." Serilda's voice trails off with a soft sadness. She continues to whisk at her bowl with intent.

Alara ignores the statement and moves to the cot where Maren lies, sweating and shaking. She points a finger at her. "You almost got yourself killed!" she spits, anger in her voice. "What the hell were you thinking?"

"I had a clear shot." Maren's voice is hoarse, the usual venom in it absent. "If you hadn't been in the way—"

"I wasn't in the way," Alara cuts her off, unwilling to cater to the idiocy. "I had control. You ran in like a fool trying to take the kill!"

"I'm not weak," Maren says quietly.

"No. But you are reckless," Alara snaps. "And you're done. You're off the hunt."

Maren turns her head towards her, wincing from the sudden movement, "You can't—"

"She can," Auryn interjects, his voice low and warning. "She's lead."

"My father will put you in your place," Maren threatens, the venom returning to her shrill voice.

Bram shakes his head grimly. "You nearly lost your leg," he adds. "You need to heal. I'm sure your father would agree."

"You know nothing about what my father would want."

Alara and Maren stare each other down, a silent war crackling between them, as Serilda continues to stir.

41

"You look just like her, you know," Serilda says, cutting the silence with her whimsical voice, her round, blue eyes still fixed on her project.

Her words land like a punch to the chest. Alara blinks, her anger faltering for a moment. She shakes her head, rejecting the statement. She turns her glare back to Maren. "You're out."

"Same fire in her spine... same... same... but entirely different," Serilda trails off, speaking to no one directly and starts mumbling into her bowl.

"I don't want to talk about her," Alara pleads.

The other hunters shift nervously at the old witch's incoherent mutterings. Never truly knowing what secrets her words hold. Never truly knowing if she is friend, or something more sinister.

"You never do. You stopped coming," Serilda replies, gentle yet accusing. "She would have hated that. But... she would have understood."

Alara doesn't answer. Maren adjusts in the thin bed holding her weight. Its creaking draws Alara's attention back to her, the tension recoiling with the familiarity of a stretched wire.

"She's out," Alara says, firmer now, addressing the other hunters. "When we move, we do it without her."

"She won't be walking for days," Auryn responds.

"She will walk," Serilda remarks. "Won't run. Won't climb. But she will walk." Her voice takes on a familiar riddle-edge as she speaks. "Broken blades can cut, when held with purpose."

"I'm not holding her," Alara says, coldly. "Not anymore." She moves towards the door. Serilda reaches out as she passes, brushing her cool fingers against her wrist, gently holding her there.

"There's a shadow in you," Serilda tells her. "It's growing teeth. Trying to get out..."

Alara doesn't reply but something odd and unfamiliar weighs in her chest. She turns her hand slightly to free herself but Serilda has already let go. Her eyes flick to the bowl the old witch has been vigorously stirring since she entered.

Empty.

Not an herb. Not a liquid. The bowl is clean and bone-dry.

Her eyes linger a moment too long. Serilda notices. She smiles at her and nods, an acknowledgment of her peculiarity.

Alara turns to leave without another word. The door creaks shut behind her, like the closing of a spell.

Alara walks through the skinny path. Vines and stinging nettle pull at her pant legs as she trudges through. When she finally reaches the main road, stares and whispers erupt behind her. She has gotten used to them now. The oblivious nature of the people around her. She ignores them as she always does.

Pillow.

The final item on her list for the day.

She stays on the main path, stopping just two cottages from her own. Deia's home. The heart of Ravenforge. She is long widowed, her children grown, passing the days with sewing and baking.

As Alara reaches the door, a warm wave of freshly baked honey-bread and cinnamon hits her, the smell teasing her nostrils. Her mouth salivates at the aroma. Alara knocks twice. The door swings open almost instantly, as though she were expected.

Deia stands in the doorway, wrapped in a flour-dusted apron. Her hair is in small tight braids, knotted at the top of her head. Her chestnut skin glows in the sunlight. She places her hands firmly on her wide hips and looks at Alara with knowing. Understanding. The thing Alara craves above all else.

"I was wondering when I'd next see you at my door," Deia says with a small smile. "Well, come on," she urges her. "I've got pastries in the oven."

Alara steps over the threshold. The smell of bread and honey wraps around her like a blanket. Her stomach answers the smell with a low, impatient growl.

A long wooden table stands in the center of the room. Bowls of flour and berry juice stains are scattered across it. It is always a chaotic welcome here.

"It's over there," Deia says, pointing to a clean, plump pillow lying on the rocking chair in the corner.

"You made me a pillow? Has Alec spoken to you?"

Deia snorts, returning to her table to knead at some dough. "No, he didn't. I thought I'd get a head start this time, child." She leans her weight into the dough with a soft grunt. "Those dreams bothering you again?"

Alara lets out a quiet exhale, "That obvious?"

"I figure that's why you're here," Deia says, sprinkling more flour atop the dough. "Or maybe you'd like a bowl of my famous stew?"

Alara nods, "I'd love some," she answers, heading to the rocking chair. She reaches for the cotton pillow, running her fingers over the stitching. She turns it over. A delicate rune has been threaded into the corner. A subtle protection against the things that wait in her nightmares.

"Where'd you learn this?" Alara asks, raising her eyebrows.

"Think you're the only one that knows how to read a book?" Deia clicks her tongue and places a small, shallow bowl on the table. "Serilda gifted me a book or two. Not sure how well that'll work, though," she says pointing to the pillow in Alara's hands. She ladles two scoops of stew from a steamy pot into the bowl she's laid out.

Alara brushes her thumb over the rune before tucking the pillow under her arm. She sits at the table and inhales the stew before her, too hungry to savour the meal. She thinks she tastes carrots and the starch of potato.

She scans the room, a habit she has built on survival. A tray sits near the window, still steaming slightly. Round golden pastries, their tops glossed with honey glaze, overflowing with a deep violet juice.

Wild berries.

"Tell me you didn't pick those from outside the fence line."

Deia doesn't look up from the dough she's shaping into thick braided loaves. "And what if I did?"

"Those berries—"

"—have been growing since before your mama was born, child." Deia interjects. "And I ain't seen 'em bite anyone yet."

"They're not safe," Alara says, pushing up from the chair she's sitting in. She steps closer to Deia, ready to give her a good scolding. "You don't know what's soaking in the soil out there. You're lucky they didn't try to root themselves in you."

Deia lets out a long, unimpressed breath through her nose. "Child, who do you think you're talking to?"

Alara freezes mid-step.

Deia dusts her hands on her apron with deliberate calmness. "I was growing herbs and dodging monsters while you were still learning to walk a straight line. *These* berries are fine," she says with authority.

Alara says nothing. Her mouth twitches, somewhere between a grimace and a smile.

Deia points a floury finger at her. "You forget your place, girl. I may not be a witch, or a hunter but I know what fear looks like dressed up as rules."

Alara blinks at this, her expression softening.

"Now," Deia huffs, turning towards the tray of pastries, "before you go scowlin' your way outta here, take some of these for the boy." She pulls a clean cloth from a nearby drawer and wraps three of the pastries with practiced hands. She slips them into a small satchel and presses it into Alara's palm. "Tell Alec they've got honey in the dough this time. And that he'd better share one with that girl I keep seein' him sneak bread to—what's her name? The one that sways."

Alara looks at her with confusion. "Lily?"

"That's the one," Deia confirms. "Tell him she might like somethin' sweet. She never eats the bread."

Alara stares for a moment at the satchel and the pillow. "You really stitched a nightmare rune for me..."

"Mm-hmm. And I baked half the village into sugar comas this week and didn't hear a single *thank you*." She winks at Alara and turns back to her baking. "But yes, I did, child."

"Alara smiles, just barely. "Thank you."

"See? Now is that so hard?" Deia chuckles. "Go on now." She waves her off. "You smell like ghosts."

Alara gives her a look, half smiling, half exhausted, as she turns to leave. The pillow tucked under one arm, the satchel in hand.

The air outside is cooler now, quieter, with very few people to pass on the way home.

Alara reaches the door. She lifts the latch and pushes it open with her shoulder, closing it behind her with her foot.

Alec is sitting by the hearth, legs crossed, drawing something in charcoal on a piece of parchment. As Alara latches the door behind her he looks up. "Is that blood?" His little voice rings with both worry and excitement.

Alara looks down at her hands. A deep rust colour has dried into the creases of her knuckles. "Yeah... But it's not mine."

"NeedleTeeth!" Alec straightens his posture, his excitement highly detectable now. Alara nods. He asks a flurry of questions before Alara has a chance to answer one. "Did you kill it? You got it, right? Did you cut its head off?"

She laughs and reaches into the satchel hanging from her shoulder, tossing him one of Deia's freshly baked pastries. "Maren almost lost her leg," she tells him.

He has already opened the satchel, peeling back the cloth from one of the berry pastries. Berries that Deia swore were safe. Alara trusts her. Besides, the berries she used were not like the forbidden ones scattered through the forest. These ones grow just beyond the fence line. They don't hum. They don't lure. They don't lie.

"Is Maren alright?" Alec asks, taking an impossibly large bite of the pastry. Violet berry juice stains his lips and fingers instantaneously.

"She'll live," Alara says, easing down into the worn chair beside him. She pats the pillow on her lap. "Clawed her leg to the bone."

He winces, mid-bite. "Ew." He chews slower, grimacing at the imagery.

"She'll be fine," Alara assures him.

"New pillow?" he says, pointing a purple-stained finger at her lap.

"Yep!" She exclaims, tossing the pillow in the air playfully. "This one might survive the night." She flips it over to reveal the rune stitched at the corner.

"Hey!" His eyes light up. "Mama used to make those on our nightgowns!" His excitement falters in an instant. His eyes fix to the treat in his hands. He shoves the last bite into his mouth and starts licking his fingers.

49

She doesn't answer. Instead, she stands, crossing the small space and dropping her pillow onto her bed. She changes the subject, saving them both from heartache. "Deia told me you've been sneaking bread to Lily,"
"She did?" He shifts nervously. "She looks hungry…"
Alara walks back to her brother. She sits beside him on the floor, crossing her legs. "They don't eat," she says gently, "but that's kind of you." She smiles at him. "She may not understand it but I think she notices." She wraps her arm around him and leans her head against his wild curls. "Bram, Auryn, and I are doing a sweep of the forest tonight. We need to bring Emalie and Isaac home."
He leans into her, wishing she could stay. "Alright…" he sighs, his shoulders slinking towards the floor.
"While I'm gone, I need you to follow the rules," she says, tousling his hair. "You don't leave the fence line. No climbing on roofs. In before dark. And if you hear someone that sounds like me, for the Gods' sake—"
"Don't follow it," he recites.
"Good." She reaches into the satchel Deia had given her, pulling out another cloth wrapped pastry. "Save this one for Lily," she says with a wink.
He blinks at her. "Really?"
Alara nods and squeezes him tightly. "She might not eat it but she might like having it." She

kisses the top of his head, his golden curls tickling her nose.

She stands and moves to her cot, sitting down slowly, trying not to put pressure on her injured shoulder. She leans back, laying her head on her new pillow. It's too firm for the moment. Not yet broken in. She turns on her side with a soft wince as the movement pulls at her.

Her gaze lands on the wall beside her. Shapes and faint lines carved in the wood. A masterpiece Alec had made for her when he was much smaller. Suns with sporadic rays and ugly stick figures with messed-up faces greet her. They're framed with tiny scratches from when Alec would sneak her blade to practice "cutting." She smiles at the memories.

Behind her she can hear Alec humming the old lullaby their mother used to sing, his attention now back to his parchment. A melody of scribbling and music fill their home.

Alara closes her eyes, still smiling.

Chapter Six

How long have I been laying like this? Did I fall asleep?

The room is quiet and dark. Alec's humming and scribbling are absent. I sit up in my bed, blinking in the darkness, willing my eyes to adjust.

"Alec?"

There's no response.

I swing my legs off the cot, standing cautiously. My home, usually full of warmth and song, feels different. Hollowed out. Empty.

Where is he?

I cross the room in slow, careful steps. The floor is cold and groans under my feet. My hand grazes the table by the door. The air feels odd in my lungs. Unwelcoming.

I need to find him.

I slide my hand along the wall, searching for the latch. My fingertips finally make contact. I swing the door open and step out.

The moon hangs low in the sky, swollen and pale. I scan the area until I spot him.

Alec.

He's standing at the fence line, speaking to someone. A woman. She's dressed in white and appears to glow in the darkness. Her face is turned away. Her hair hangs damp and straight, like wet separated threads. They're speaking.

What are they saying?

I see Alec reach out to her. He takes her hand.

No.

"Alec!" He doesn't hear me.

He follows her, his small feet patting into the dirt as he leaves with her. Into the woods. She doesn't tug him. He walks willingly.

I run after them, barefoot. The earth feels soft. Like it's giving way, resisting me. I reach the trees. They are pressed in too tightly, suffocating me as I push through them. Branches tangle in my hair and claw at my clothes. I call for him again but no sound comes out.

The forest is endless. A labyrinth of trees at every step. I can't navigate it. I don't know this place. I wander around, aimlessly. An unfamiliar tree stands as an obstacle at every turn.

I can't find him.

I'm about to give up, exhausting my search, battered by trees that don't belong. That's when I hear it. Two voices. Alec's and mine. But I'm not speaking. My heart sinks.

"Alec! That's not me!" I cry out.

There's no answer. Only the lilt of my own voice, moving deeper into the woods. It's soft and motherly, mixed with something sinister.

I break through the last of the trees, coming to a clearing. I stop.

They're sitting near the old creek bed. My peaceful place. Alec... and me.

No.

She wears my face but it isn't mine. Her hair is wet and muddy, hanging over her back and shoulders. She looks like she has just climbed out of a wet grave. Her eyes glow faintly in the dark. She's smiling a smile I have never worn. Too sweet, too big. She strokes his curls gently, as if she's always been the one to soothe him. He leans into her.

"Alec! Get away from it!"

I rush forward, stumbling, reaching for my brother. He doesn't notice me. But *she* does. Her eyes meet my own. Her smile widens.

"Don't worry," she says in my voice. "I'll take care of him." She starts to hum. She kneels in the shallows, water rippling around her. She beckons for him to join her.

He does.

I try to move but my legs sink into the earth, capturing me there. Unrelenting.

"Alec, stop!"

She cups his cheeks in her hands, gently tilting his face to hers. Her expression is soft and loving. She leans in and pushes him under the water.

"No! Let him go!" I scream. I can't move. I can't get to him.

The water splashes, thrashes, and bubbles. Alec's limbs flail beneath the surface, small and desperate. She continues to hum while holding him under with terrifying stillness. Her smile never falters.

"Get off him!" I beg. She doesn't let up. I scream until my voice gives out. I can't help him.

He goes still. His little hands drift limp, his head now bobbing in the creek. The humming stops.

"You see?" She says, rising from the water. "He belongs with *us*."

I can move now. The earth releases its hold on me. I fall onto my back, sobbing silently. There's something behind me. I can feel the heat. I turn, slow and shaking.

It stands there, wreathed in darkness, towering over me.

Let me out.

"Alara?" Alec calls to her, his voice tugging her back from the dark woods.

Her eyes snap open to find him sitting on her bed, his brows pinched with concern. Light pours through the tattered curtains. The sun is high. She sits up. "Alec..." she grabs him, pulling him into a tight hug on her lap. She presses her cheek into his hair, anchoring herself to the waking world.

"You were crying," he tells her. He wipes at her wet cheeks.

"Bad dream," she sighs, releasing her grip on him. "And bad news." She slaps the rune on the pillow beside her. "This doesn't work."

"Maybe Deia didn't do it right," he offers. He drops his head. "Mama knew how..."

"Mama knew a lot of things," she says, brushing a hand on his cheek. "That's why we're so smart." She pokes his nose with her index finger. She kisses his forehead and gives him one last squeeze before gently shifting him off her lap. She pushes off the bed and stretches her arms up to the ceiling. "Stay inside, alright?" she says, heading towards the chest beside the hearth.

Alec watches her as she opens the lid and begins rummaging through the chest, gathering supplies. Charcoal, iron shavings, matches. She places them in a small leather bag and slings it over her shoulder. Her dagger follows. She straps it to her thigh.

"Do you think Emalie and Isaac are okay?" He asks, concern flooding his delicate voice.

56

She pauses and turns to him. She's not quite sure what to say. He looks to her for answers about his missing friends and she's desperate to provide them. But the forest isn't safe for any of Ravenforge's people and the truth is that the children don't stand much of a chance out there alone. She bends down to match his height. "I hope so," she whispers. "I'll bring them home, either way."

She can tell this brings him no comfort. He doesn't look at her. He moves across the room and sits himself beside his drawings. He continues to scribble.

Alara sighs as she rises to her feet, giving him one last pat on the head before turning towards the door. "I won't be long," she says as she moves the latch. "I promise."

He doesn't answer. He is too focused on his parchment. His tongue pokes out at the corner of his mouth. A habit he has always had.

She opens the door, leaving before he can see the sadness creeping across her face.

Alara crouches at the end of the eastern fence, pressing charcoal into the wood. Her strokes are steady and practiced—tight spirals and broken slashes, marks drawn with intent. She sprinkles a fine line of iron shavings at the base of the posts and strikes a match. The flame flares, igniting the charcoal. She whispers a quiet incantation under her breath, activating the sigil, before dusting off her fingers and moving to the next post.

"Talking to the fence again?"

Her eyes stay fixed on the wood. "Still hovering like a stray dog?" she says, striking another match.

Auryn steps into view. An axe is strapped to his back and a rusty canteen hangs from his belt. He leans against the fence, taking a look at her work. "Bram thought you took off. I figured you'd be doing your burn-anything-that-breathes-wrong routine."

She finishes the next post. "I'm glad someone listens."

"I always listen."

Alara's throat tightens. The charcoal in her hand stills. The statement strikes her harder than it should.

The memory edges in before she can shove it away. The two of them, young and circling each other in the barracks, bare feet on the stone floor. Their wooden blades clashing against each other. The echo of their laughter when she would land a strike. The teasing grin he would wear when he would sweep her legs, dropping her flat on her back. The sting of bruises... The fire of pride. Sweating and bleeding together was their game.

Alara sprinkles the last bit of iron, lights the sigil, and straightens. "There," she says. "I'm done."

"Hopefully your angry little symbols will light 'em up before they can cause any more damage."

"That's the idea."

Auryn's gaze stays on her a moment longer than necessary. "I saw that girl again earlier. The dead one. What's her name?"

"Lily."

"Yeah... Lily," he laughs. "Cause of the lilies on her dress?"

"You got a better name for her?" Alara challenges.

He pushes off the fence. "Yeah, actually... Scab... that dead girl." He smiles at her. She doesn't react. He notices. "You check on her lately?" he asks, his voice softer now.

"I always do," Alara says, walking along the fence, following the dirt path to the main tree line.

"Does she talk to you or somethin'?"

"She's a Scab." She shoots a look in his direction. "She can't speak."

Auryn snorts. "And you're still out there, visiting her. You know most of us avoid dead people. And then there's you, making friends with one."

"She's not dead."

"She's not lively, either," Auryn mutters.

"She's gentle. She doesn't hurt anyone," she says, stepping over a branch in her path.

"So is a stump. But a stump is easier to look at." He chuckles to himself.

She stops walking and turns to face him. "Why do you care?"

"I don't. Not really."

She gives him a dry look. "Then what's your point?"

He shrugs. Alara narrows her eyes at him and turns around, dodging more wind-swept branches. "I just think," she rolls her eyes as he continues, "if you put half as much effort into talking to the living... you might actually make a friend or two."

Alara raises her brows, still pushing her way through the scattered sticks. "Are you offering?"

"I'm excellent company," Auryn beams without missing a beat. "Ask no one." She smiles faintly and continues on her way. Auryn follows closely behind her. "You should teach us," he says, quickening his pace to match hers. He falls in step beside her. "How to do the sigils, I mean."

She shakes her head and scrunches her nose. "I'm no teacher."

"You could be. If you didn't hate people so much," he teases.

"I don't hate people," Alara replies. "I just don't like how cruel they are... about things they don't understand."

"It's easier for us... *I* think so anyway. We know what's out there. Most of them are still stuck in the past. Praying to Gods that don't exist," Auryn's eyes scan the forest as they reach the meeting point. The trees arch in a twisted canopy,

60

roots like outstretched fingers, inviting the unwise to wander in and lose their way. "Sometimes I envy the others... They don't have to see the things we see. Do the things we have to..." he trails off.

"They're the lucky ones," Alara says, honestly.

"Maybe... But just so you know, you're not the only one they talk about," he mutters, nudging her arm. *The kind of thing friends do.* Auryn watches her as they walk. He looks at her more directly, like he's been mulling something over and has finally decided to speak of it. "The NeedleTeeth that injured Maren... Can they all do what it did?"

"I'm not sure," she answers. "That was the first I've seen." A cold ripple moves beneath her skin, mimicking the unbearable ice that dragged over her bones as the NeedleTeeth passed through her. She gags at the taste it left in her throat. A shudder rolls over her. "At least now we will be prepared. If it ever happens again..."

Up ahead, Bram stands with his back to them, one foot planted on a mossy log. He draws a whetstone along his blade in steady strokes. The soft rasp of scraping metal echoes through the trees. "Took you long enough," he says, without turning to them, rhythmically sharpening the steel.

Alara stops a few paces away. "Nice to see you too."

Auryn drops the axe from his back for a quick relief of the weight. It lands with a soft thud. "We weren't sightseeing. She was finishing the wards."

Bram glances over his shoulder, just enough to show he's listening. "They'll hold?"

"Long enough for us to get back. If it doesn't rain," Alara answers.

"Good." Bram finishes the pass of the whetstone, sets it aside, and wipes the blade on the hem of his shirt. "We should move out. I need to get back to my mother and we're losing sun."

Chapter Seven

By the time the hunters return to Ravenforge, the sun has dipped low behind the trees. The light bleeds gold and rust through the branches, casting long, finger-like shadows across the field. The dusky glow feels heavy, the air cooled. The wind brushes their skin with a quiet edge. Disappointment hangs in the stillness. It lingers in their footsteps. No one speaks as they cross the warded fence.

Their search had stretched for hours—through gullies, shallow tunnels made by wildlife, and deer paths—but in the end, it led nowhere. Just old animal tracks, clawed up trees, and the hush of the forest. No NeedleTeeth. No children. Nothing. They return empty-handed.

As they move past the fence, they see him.

Waiting.

Councilman Thomas.

He stands alone, bottle clutched in hand, coat stained and unevenly buttoned. His face is flushed with drink, eyes glassy and red-rimmed. He sways slightly, as though the ground is shifting under his feet.

Auryn sighs under his breath. "Of course."

Thomas doesn't wait for them to reach him. He storms forward, boots dragging, as he continues to stumble in their direction. His words come loud and sharp, forced through slurred teeth. "You left my daughter with *Serilda,*" he bellows, hanging on the name, spitting the foul taste of it from his lips. "You dropped her in that witch's shack like a dying animal!"

"Would you rather I let her bleed out? Lose her leg?" Alara replies calmly, meeting his glare without flinching. "Serilda is the only healer who can treat a wound to that degree."

"She's home now," he slurs. He points a long, white finger at her, "And *you* cannot keep her off this hunt. The council has final say."

Auryn takes a step towards him, placing himself in the middle of the exchange. "If you plan on bringing this up with the council, do it sober."

Something flickers in Thomas's eyes. Anger that slowly festers as he wobbles in place. "She's a hunter. She needs to be out in the fields."

"How?" Alara asks. "Have you seen her leg? Did you even check the damage?"

"The *witch* says she'll walk by morning," Thomas spits. "*You* don't get to make that call." He takes another step towards Alara and raises the bottle to his lips, his knuckles white from the tension.

Bram steps forward now, putting his hand out to ensure the old drunk stays where he is. "That's close enough, Thomas. You can hardly stand straight. Go home before this turns into something you can't handle."

Thomas stares at him, unmoving. He staggers in place, the bottle still held tightly in his hand. He takes one last look at Alara. "You're just like her, y'know," he says, as if his words carry insult. "You even wear her face. Should've known you'd be just as righteous. And look where that got *her*," he laughs cruelly.

"Watch it." There's anger in Auryn's voice now as he moves closer to the inebriated fool. "Turn around. Go home."

The wind sweeps up the thin threads of Thomas's white greased hair, making them dance in a crazed fashion. "Maren will be on the next search." He pivots on legs that tremble beneath him and stumbles off, clutching his bottle like a prized possession. Curses trail behind him as he staggers back to the village.

Bram runs a hand through his hair. "He's worse when he drinks."

"Which is everyday…" Auryn states with a roll of his eyes. "He'll stir the council."

Bram lets out a low grunt as he starts walking towards the cottages. Alara and Auryn follow in step. "Hopefully, he's too full of drink to remember."

"Not likely with Maren at home," Alara says. "He'll be angrier in the morning."

"That's a problem for tomorrow," Bram replies, the tired bags under his eyes practically swallowing his cheeks. "We should try to get some proper sleep. We will have to deal with the council in the morning. They will want to know about tonight's sweep."

They walk in silence, the weight of the search's failure pressing into every step. Their pace is slow, deliberate, as if dragging their heels might delay the reckoning of tomorrow. The morning will come and with it, questions and accusations. The hunters returned. The children did not.

A soft, metallic sound rises from the stillness.

DingDingDing

It rings out across the square from the far side of the village, delicate but distinct.

Bram's body stiffens beside his fellow hunters before it finishes its echo. The noise cuts straight through him. "Her bell," he whispers to himself. He lifts his eyes to meet the others and opens his mouth to speak.

"Go," Alara interrupts without hesitation. "Your mother needs you."

"She's been ringing that bell a lot less these days," he stammers, scratching the back of his neck. "The sickness is getting weaker. But we've been gone a while. She probably needs help to the bathroom or something."

Alara nods slowly. "It's fine. We'll pick up the search tomorrow."

He doesn't wait for anything more. He breaks into a run, his footsteps receding quickly into the darkened streets, kicking up dust as he moves towards the familiar sound that anchors him home.

Alara and Auryn trail behind him. They reach the edge of the fields and Auryn veers off, moving too slowly to his home on the main path. He nods to her, hardly lifting his head through his exhaustion. Alara smiles back at him, flicking her wrist with a lazy half-wave, before she reaches the threshold of her own cottage.

She stands there for a moment, listening to the forest. She listens to the wind threading through stalks. To the swaying of the trees in the distance. To nothing at all.

She closes her eyes and imagines it—a miracle she knows won't come. A laugh. A cry. The sound of small feet breaking through the trees. The nightmare ending for the mothers and fathers that keep a lit candle in their windows.

But no voice comes. No footsteps. Only stillness.

The forest doesn't give anything back. It only takes.

The quiet presses in tighter as the wind stops. She opens her eyes and moves for the latch but freezes when she hears something shift behind her. Not violently but there's a soft disturbance in the air. It's not wind. It's intentional. Something is moving in the forest behind her.

She turns towards the sound. Past the grain fields and the old fence, something slips through the trees. A glint of black and silver. Its movement is too smooth to be walking. Too fast to be human. She narrows her eyes, trying to get a better look at it. It moves like it belongs to the forest, as if the trees make room for it and close behind it just as quickly.

Alara doesn't reach for her blade. She watches the colours dance and glide, before they disappear altogether. Gone before she can make sense of it. She can feel her heart racing. Her breath quickens as she scans the trees. Something is out there. Watching.

The people of Ravenforge are cautious. For good reason. There are things that live in the forest far worse than the NeedleTeeth. Things that smile. Things that don't bleed. Things that can't die.

When the colours don't return and the silence lingers, she lifts the latch and steps inside, securing the door behind her with a turn of the iron lock. The bolt slides home with a sound too soft to feel like protection but the stories say the worst ones—the ones that never blink, cannot enter a home uninvited. And in Ravenforge, whispers and stories often hold true.

    Alara leans her forehead against the door and listens to Alec's soft snoring, coming from the far corner of the room. It drifts through the cottage delicately. She breathes shallow and quiet, not to disturb her little brother. He deserves a good night's sleep.
    She turns, pushing her back against the door. The room is dim and warm. The embers glow through the shadows. Alec's charcoal drawings lay scattered by the hearth, the wrapping from Deia's berry pastries crumpled on the floor.
    Alara slowly walks over to the mess, picking up the drawings and wrapping, gently tapping the parchments and laying them evenly on the table. She tosses the wrapping into the embers, watching as they catch fire and turn to ash just as quickly. She eases herself to the floor, curling around the fireplace, trying to soak up the last bit of heat it has to offer. The wood beneath her is still hot. Alara presses her injured shoulder to it, sighing in relief at the warmth. Her eyes close and for once, she doesn't fight sleep. She welcomes it.

    Alara drifts between sleep and alert throughout the night, never fully surrendering.

Never dropping her guard enough to get the rest her body desperately craves.

Visions of a dimly lit hallway flash through her head, a deep creeping snore bouncing off the walls around her. Her eyes flutter open for a brief moment before the faded dream takes hold of her again.

An empty crib. The sense of panic enveloping the sight.

Her mother's song drifts through the space. She tries to seek out the source but finds herself in another place altogether.

A cold barn. Overwhelming sadness seeping through the straws of hay. An impossibly tiny body thrown carelessly on the heap.

Anger.

Betrayal.

Alara's body jolts and her eyes snap open at the sensation of a lengthy fall. One name whispers through her mind as her vision begins to focus.

Aveline.

She shakes her head from the distorted dream. The sun has risen, casting beams through the crooked window.

She stirs, muscles stiff from the cold hard floor. Her body aches in a deep, marrow-heavy way that comes after too many nights of too little rest.

Something brushes against her face. It tickles her chin. She opens her eyes, blinking against the sun.

Hair. Wild, untamed curls.

Alec.

He's tucked against her chest, one arm thrown over her waist. A pillow is wedged beneath her head. Alec's blanket lies unevenly across her leg. She looks down at him. His lashes fan over his cheeks, his lips slightly parted, a dribble of drool clinging to them. She doesn't move, refusing to disturb him and the peace the moment brings to her. She lifts her hand and gently brushes his hair behind his tiny ear, running her finger over the freckle beside it.

Three sharp raps at the door shatter the tenderness of the moment. Alec shifts against her, frowning in his sleep. She stays lying on the floor, holding her brother, not wanting to let go.

Just one more minute.

Another knock, louder this time.

She exhales and eases Alec onto the pillow, slowly and carefully, as if a swift movement would cause him to break. Her body protests but she pushes herself to her feet. She ignores it, already walking to the door, her bones cold with exhaustion.

She slides the lock and unlatches it. It opens with a faint creek.

Auryn stands in the doorway, slightly leaning against the frame. "Morning."

"Barely," Alara mutters, rubbing the sleep out of her eyes.

He glances past her, finding Alec lying on the floor. "Let him sleep," he says, voice low. He tips his head away from her, signalling for her to step outside. She does, latching the door behind her.

The chill from the morning air hits first, clean and biting. Mist coils around their ankles, wrapping around them like snakes, willing themselves into existence. A raven cries off in the distance.

She leans with him on the frame, crossing her arms. "Let me guess…"

He nods, answering the question she has yet to ask. "The Council has called a meeting."

She rolls her eyes and shakes her head. "As expected. Thomas's doing, no doubt."

"Yep. He's pushing hard. He wants Maren reinstated." His gaze falls to the ground. "And they want to discuss the children. What we should do next…"

Alara furrows her brow. "They think they're dead."

He meets her eyes. She catches the guilt and sadness buried in his own. "It's been three days, Alara…"

Alara doesn't answer. Her eyes drift to the forest's edge. It waits at the end of the fields. Standing tall. Engulfed in morning mist, shadowed by the rising sun. It's still. Quiet. It lies.

Three days.

She remembers when her mother went missing... She remembers the search parties thinning out after the first night. On the second, people stopped meeting her eyes when she'd ask if they'd heard anything. Elder Tilda would not answer as she begged her for just one more day, just one more sweep. On the third day, they stopped going. They stopped calling her name. They stopped hoping.

At just sixteen years old, Alara had decided to find her on her own. Pushing any fear or doubt out of her mind. Clinging to her mission. To hope. To bringing Lyssa home. For her. For Alec. For her people. Alara clung to the fantasy.

Her mother was not gone, only lost. She would find her, hungry and dehydrated no doubt but she'd be in one piece. And Lyssa would be so happy to see her daughter. She would be so proud. She would talk for years about how, when Ravenforge lost all hope, her daughter never did.

She set off one night, alone. She tucked Alec into bed. He had been crying himself to sleep every night their mother did not return. She had kissed him and promised when he woke in the morning their mother would be there. He hugged her so tightly that night, truly believing in his older sister.

She remembers the frost biting at her fingers, how her legs shook as she searched the forest, calling to her mother. She remembers slipping down the slope into the ravine, clothes soaked, hands torn from clawing through brush. She remembers the quiet and the way her mother's body looked, crumpled at the bottom of the pit. Her body had been torn open, her organs chewed, her face bloated and almost unrecognisable. She remembers her eyes, the sockets hollow with shallow pinpoint pricks around them, as though they had been pecked out. Her jaw hung open, frozen in the echo of an eternal scream... The floor around her was black. Wet. An undeniable sick-sweet scent hung in the air. She remembers trying to close her mother's mouth through her anguished sobs, trying to clean her face with her shirt. The flies were feasting as she waved them off the body, again and again, frantically whispering spells and incantations, desperate to undo what had been done.

Alara draws in a long, shaky breath, closing her eyes tightly, denying her memories. Her fists are clenched at her side, her nails digging into her skin. "We won't abandon them." she finally says, her voice betraying her as it quivers. Auryn watches her, knowing better than to interrupt. "If they *are* dead," she continues, eyes still locked on the forest, "they're still coming home." She blinks back the sting of a tear.

Auryn doesn't speak right away. He steps closer and rests a hand on her shoulder—not heavily, not hesitant. Just enough to let her know she's not alone. "We'll bring them home," he finally says. He gives her shoulder the slightest squeeze before letting go. "One way or another."

Chapter Eight

The doors to the old chapel groan as Alara pushes through. Auryn stays close to her side. The meeting is already underway as they enter. Elder Tilda sits at the head of the room at the old altar, her cane resting across her lap. She sits tall, too straight for her age. Councilwoman Elowen sits to her left, hands folded, eyes sharp beneath her hood. On the other side of Elder Tilda sits Councilman Thomas. He's in rough shape—eyes rimmed red, face puffed from a night of drink. His collar hangs loose. He's forgotten to button it through the hangover. His expression tightens as Alara steps inside.

Bram leans against a support beam near the wall. His face remains as drawn and tired as the previous night. He doesn't meet their eyes but Alara spots a feather-light shift in his jaw as they appear.

Maren stands beside him, braced on both legs, clearly favouring one over the other. Her face is unreadable—an odd occurrence as she usually wears her disdain proudly.

Thomas speaks. "It's a fool's errand at this point. No tracks. No sounds. Nothing to report back. The forest has taken them. We waste time and risk lives by chasing ghosts."

There is a muffled sob at the back of the room. Emalie's mother. She buries her face in her husband's arm, stifling her anguish.

"No," Alara's voice cuts through the chamber. Heads turn at the sound.

Thomas glares her way, "You speak out of turn, girl."

Elder Tilda ignores the accusation and places her hand in front of her, beckoning Alara forward. "Come, child." Alara moves to the old altar, stopping before her. "Speak, if you have something to say."

"We've found no bodies. No NeedleTeeth. No new tracks. This is true," she says. She turns towards the people of Ravenforge now, looking to the mourning parents in the crowd. "But we've also found no reason to stop looking. Emalie and Isaac are out there and if there's any chance they're still alive," she turns to Thomas, "the search must go on. With or without your council."

Elder Tilda, Councilwoman Elowen, and Thomas whisper amongst each other before returning their attention back to Alara.

"We will extend the search by one day," Tilda says. Alara nods at this, gratefully. "Now, we must address the final matter. Maren, step forward, dear."

Maren stiffens at the sudden attention, seemingly caught off guard. She recovers quickly, lifting her chin and stepping forward with practiced composure. Her limp is masked well but Alara knows better.

Every step sends a ripple of tension through her shoulders but she refuses to drop her eyes. She halts before the table, stopping beside Alara, her back too straight to appear natural.

Thomas watches with crossed arms, his expression bearing pride and expectation.

Tilda observes silently for a moment. "I see you can walk." She studies her from boots to brow, searching her for weakness. "Can you fight, if need be?"

Maren nods with confidence. "I will fight until my last breath."

"Very well. Four hunters are greater than three," Tilda remarks. "You shall go today with the others."

A disbelieving laugh escapes Alara's lips. "She can *barely* walk," she says. "You expect her to do anything but slow us down? She's a liability."

"I will gladly lay my life down if it comes to that," Maren replies, her eyes falling to the floor.

"A hunter's duty. As many have done before her," Thomas adds, his tone obnoxiously boisterous, as if he'd be proud to lose his daughter to such a cause.

Alara shakes her head, refusing the decision. She scans the room, her eyes instinctively landing on Auryn. He leans against the wall beside the old wooden doors. Their eyes meet with the same contempt to the judgment. The chamber falls silent, until the doors swing open, creaking loudly at the disturbance. Auryn steps aside to avoid getting hit, the disdain in his eyes replaced by confusion when he sees her.

Serilda.

She's barefoot, walking atop the cold stone floors, as though temperature holds no merit. Mud clings to her ankles. Her dress is soaked down to the hem, water darkening the floor as she strides through the pews. Her lips move, seemingly without sound at first, like she's mid conversation with someone no one else can see.

No one speaks. No one moves.

Her voice begins to grow. "Too many doors. Too many keys. Too many eyes. Too many teeth." Villagers try to avoid the scene. Many fail, turning their heads to the immortal woman, the strength of their curiosity overpowering them. They look away just as quickly as they catch sight of her. A silence washes over the room, some looking to the exit, mapping their escape. She continues to mutter. Women pull their shawls tighter around themselves. Men try to appear unbothered. Someone clears their throat, a little too loudly.

"The blood sings. The blood calls. The blood... blood..." Serilda continues to move between the pews, her eyes flicking around the room wildly.

Until her vision land on Alara. She stops walking. Her head tilts to one side, playfully. "When she bled, he cried. When she hums, he listens," she says in a voice too soft, through a sweet smile. The room tightens around her as she glides to an open seat. The already seated villagers scoot away from her, distancing themselves from the madness.

Thomas, usually unmovable, clears his throat and adjusts in his chair. "This is a civilized meeting," he says, though his comment lands on deaf ears. Serilda turns into her cloak and continues to whisper to herself.

The room, just moments ago tense with debate, now feels brittle, like it might splinter from the weight of simply acknowledging the witch.

Tilda speaks at last, ignoring the presence that has stirred her people to the bone. "You have one more day. All *four* of you," she says, raising a brow at Alara, expecting her bite. Alara doesn't speak.

When she hums, he listens.

80

Surely Serilda's crazed mutterings are just that. Though they do feel uncomfortably targeted. Alara takes a moment to compose herself before she answers. "Then we move, now. While we still have a full day of sun."

Maren doesn't speak but her jaw tightens and a shaky breath escapes her lips, so quietly only Alara notices.

"Very well," Tilda's voice rings out once more, final and firm. "We meet again tomorrow morning."

Alara holds the elder's gaze. A quiet acknowledgment. No words. No bow. Just a pause, long enough to say she's heard and that she'll come. She turns and walks towards the doors, her boots echoing once more over the stone floor. She's nearly fled when she feels it—that prickle at the nape of her neck. She glances over her shoulder. Serilda has turned herself in her seat. She's smiling at Alara. The same sweet smile she always wears for her.

Alara nods to her. The witch rises and follows her out of the chapel. The room can finally breathe.

They walk together towards Serilda's cottage, Alara playing the role of dutiful niece, bringing her strange aunt back home. Serilda is still muttering under her breath.

"The blood...the bl—"

"Auntie, what are you rambling about?"

Serilda's hand shoots out, catching Alara's wrist with startling strength. Her grip is tight, almost bruising. "The girl should not go," she says, eyes wide. "She should not—"

Alara stiffens. "Serilda..."

The witch blinks, clarity creeping back into her eyes, waking her from the trance. Her eyes drop to Alara's arm. Her fingers loosen. She pulls back, horrified with herself. "I'm so sorry, my dear," she whispers, frantically petting Alara's arm where she had just gripped her.

Alara doesn't flinch. She exhales slowly and steps towards Serilda, wrapping a comforting arm around her shoulder. "Come on," Alara says, "let's get you home." Alara leads her to the overgrown trail, carefully guiding her around the stinging nettle. "You forgot your shoes again, Auntie." Serilda leans into her as they continue. Her lips never stop moving.

"He watches from the fence. Shhh! Quiet! It doesn't matter..." She turns her face so her lips are close to her ear. "He can smell the blood," Serilda breathes.

Alara says nothing in return. She keeps walking, guiding Serilda, steady and protective.

"The girl hums... she hums and they listen... so many ears. So many teeth..."

Serilda's crooked house rises ahead, half-swallowed by creeping vines, slouched with age.

Alara helps her up the steps, past the dangling bones and dead garden and opens the door.

"The blood... the blood sings..."

Chapter Nine

Alec is already awake when Alara returns home. He hovers near the hearth, his curls wild from sleep. His tunic hangs lopsided over one shoulder. Alara reaches for the comb on the shelf beneath the cracked mirror. She lowers herself to the floor, patting the empty space beside her. Alec sits. She starts combing through his nest of hair.

"How was the meeting?" he asks.

"Boring," she answers, tugging the comb through a stubborn knot. Alec winces. "I'm going back out today."

Alec's head drops. "You didn't find them last night?"

She doesn't answer, continuing to sift through the mess atop his head.

"They're probably dead," Alec says plainly.

84

Alara stops combing and peers around his side to get a good look at his face. His eyes are to the floor, his brows furrowed. "We don't know that, Bub," she tells him. "I'll find them. I'll bring them home."

"You said that last time..."

She takes a moment to herself before giving him a squeeze around his shoulders. "We can't know until we know," she replies. She kisses the top of his head and continues to sort out his hair. "And if I don't know, I won't stop looking."

"At least you can bring their bodies back for their parents."

Alara runs the comb through one last time before scooping Alec up into her lap. "Don't think that way," she breathes. "There's nothing wrong with having hope."

Alec leans into her, burying his face under her chin. She holds him like that for a while, rocking him from side to side, humming into his hair.

Alara reluctantly breaks the moment. "You should visit Deia today." She lifts him as she stands and places him on his feet. "Maybe you can convince her to make you more of those pastries."

There's a flicker behind his eyes but he tries to play it off, masking the glint of excitement from detection. "Yeah... maybe."

"I'll be back before sundown," she says, planting a kiss on his forehead. He nods and throws his arms around her waist, holding on to her for as long as he can. She pulls back enough to meet his eyes. "I'll find them," she promises.

He doesn't say anything. He nods silently and steps away from the embrace. She gathers her things and reaches for the door.

Outside the mist still clings to the earth, refusing to release. Alara meets the three hunters at the clearing of the forest. They move together in uneasy silence. Bram walks ahead. Auryn stays close to Alara's side, his eyes constantly scanning the treetops. Maren lags behind, her limp subtle yet present. No one speaks until she stumbles.

"Careful," Alara says without looking back.

"I'm fine," Maren mutters, quickly regaining her footing.

Alara scoffs. "Could have fooled me."

"If you're trying to humiliate me, it's not working," Maren spits, venom in her voice.

"Oh, you humiliate yourself all on your own," Alara snaps.

Maren trips again, Auryn offers his arm to stop the fall. She begrudgingly takes it and straightens herself out. Auryn glances sideways at Alara but says nothing.

Bram calls from ahead, "If we want to cover more ground, we will have to pick up the pace."

"That's a great idea," Alara chimes. She turns towards Maren. "You want to *prove* yourself?"

Maren studies her before responding, unsure of what she's getting herself into. "I'm here, aren't I?"

"Great. Then let's cover more ground." Alara turns to Auryn and Bram who have both stopped walking. "We'll split up."

Auryn takes a deep breath. "Alara..."

"No," she holds a hand up to him. "The council has deemed her fit to be here. Who are we to decide she's not?" She turns back to Maren. "What do you think?"

"We would be able to search further if we split," Bram agrees.

Maren tips her chin upwards. "Sounds good to me. Anything to be rid of you for a while."

Alara narrows her eyes. She turns her attention to the other two. "We'll meet back at the clearing at sunset."

"I'll take the north edge, near the mountains," Bram says, already setting off down the path.

"Maren, take the west ridge. Shouldn't be an issue since you're *fine*," Alara challenges.

Maren doesn't falter. "You got it." She hisses out the words, jaw tight as ever and veers off on her own.

Alara is wearing a smug smile as she turns back to Auryn. There's no mistaking the disapproval in his eyes. "What?"

He shakes his head but doesn't answer the question. "I'll take east," he says, heading into the trees. They swallow him, leaving Alara alone.

Alara moves through the forest, towards the creek. Her blade stays loose in her grip. The trees press in close around her until she reaches the water. She crosses it, soaking her boots in the process. She hums softly, a tune without words, a half-remembered lullaby. The melody spreads through the open space like bait. And something takes it. The air around her stirs, subtle yet abruptly sharp.

"I was hoping to get you alone," calls an unfamiliar voice.

Alara's eyes flick to a nearby tree. He leans against it, arms crossed, as though he's been waiting for her. He's tall, with hair the colour of pale gold—wind swept in an intentional mess. It suits him. His skin is almost luminous in the sunlight. His eyes are an impossible icy blue. A smile tugs at his mouth, lips curving just enough to reveal two charming dimples at his cheeks.

She lifts her blade. "Don't move."

He raises an eyebrow. "Already? We've barely just met." He looks her over, his eyes scanning her, slowly. Too slowly. "Though I guess I should have expected nothing less." Alara doesn't flinch. She holds her blade firmly.

He laughs, a quiet rich laugh. "That was a lovely song," he says, pushing off the tree. He steps towards her, quickly closing the gap between them. Too quickly.

Her blade slices at his ribs but he dodges the attack. He's fast but not fast enough. The steel grazes his side, slicing through fabric and skin, before plunging into the air. The dagger ignites faintly on impact. He flinches, more with surprise than pain. "Interesting."

She follows up with a kick that slams him back to the trees. He catches himself almost effortlessly. She closes the distance and goes in for another strike. He grabs at her wrist, mid-swing and twists her arm behind her back, knocking the dagger out of her hand. He pins her against the nearest tree.

"If I wanted you dead, you'd already be a corpse," he breathes into her neck, inhaling deeply.

She shudders unwillingly and whips her head backwards, slamming into his chin. He lets go of her and staggers a couple paces back. Alara spins away fast, blade back in her hand the moment she's freed. He wipes the blood from his lip, chuckling at the sight of it.

Steel flashes towards his throat. He dodges, barely. The second slash tears through his sleeve and into his flesh. Blood darkens the light fabric. She continues to press the attack, slicing, cutting, and spinning, seemingly all at once. He's faster now, ducking and dodging each move she makes. He catches her wrist again, twisting it. The knife flies from her hand. She grunts against the pain but continues to fight, throwing a knee into his side. He absorbs the hit, gritting his teeth. He lets out a low growl and his hand shoots out, gripping the front of her shirt. She has no time to react before he slams her backwards into a tree. The bark splits and her breath leaves her in a rush. She stays there, gasping once—twice, trying to pull air back into her lungs as though she's drowning. He holds her there, his eyes tracing the panic blooming across her features. He smiles and releases her, putting out his hands, palms first in surrender. He steps away as she continues to gasp, composing herself.

 He watches her, blood trailing down his arm, soaking the cuff of his sleeve. Alara's eyes land on her dagger. It lays in the grass on the other side of the stranger. She decides to keep her distance. His eyes stay on her, locked and analyzing.

 "Tapping out? Clever girl." He winks at her, that same arrogant smirk returning to his lips.

 "What are you?" she asks, her chest still rising and falling without rhythm. She tracks the blade in the grass, as though it might sprout wings and fly away.

 He shrugs. "Just another creature in these woods."

 "What do you want?"

 "I haven't decided that yet," he says. He follows her gaze, then bends and plucks the dagger from the earth. He spins it through his fingers with lazy precision. Casual—mocking her, before he stills it in his palm. "This is a neat little thing," he muses, throwing around the steel again, playfully. "You don't see hexed steel outside of coven circles these days. Don't see many covens, either."

He strides towards her, flipping the blade once more. Her throat tightens but Alara doesn't back away. Her spine still aches from the slam to the bark but she doesn't let it show. She squares her stance, unsure of what her next move is. Unsure of what *his* next move is. She forces her expression blankly, though every step he takes makes her heart thump into her ribs. He stops closely before her. Too close. She could strike him. He could easily use her own blade against her. As she's mentally preparing for another attack he holds the dagger out to her, hilt first.

He smiles at her hesitation. "A peace offering," he tells her.

Her fingers twitch but she doesn't reach for it. Not yet. She doesn't trust the ease in his stance or the quiet in his voice. She doesn't trust his angelic face or playful demeanour. She doesn't trust him standing this close, smiling at her as though none of this matters.

He waves the blade at her, seemingly getting annoyed with holding it. She snatches it. Her hand closes around the hilt. She holds it between them like a barrier.

He chuckles softly and continues to watch her. "You always breathe like this after a fight?" She doesn't dignify the comment with a response.

He continues to study her, making her skin crawl with his eyes. Alara keeps her spine straight but every nerve in her body feels stretched thin. Her heart refuses to settle. She fights off the urge to run, refusing to give him the satisfaction. His stare remains lingering, flicking between her neck and her eyes. Her fingers squeeze the hilt of her dagger, ready to drive it through his jaw.

Something shifts in him. His gaze cuts to the side. His posture adjusts, the way a predator listens to coming prey. He angles his head slightly. "You've got company," he whispers, raising his brows at her with another smirk. "We'll continue this another time, huntress."

He's gone before she can draw in another breath. Only the space where he stood remains. She forces her hand to unclench from the hilt, thumb brushing over the grooves of the runes, grounding herself from the strange interaction.

A blunt sound breaks through the quiet. Footsteps. They are rushing towards her. She readies her dagger. "Alara!" She sighs in relief at the familiar voice and sheaths her blade.

Auryn pushes through the brush. He stands at the creek bed opposite her. His eyes scan her briefly, his brows furrowing. "Are you alright?"

"Fine," she tells him.

He doesn't push. Instead, he holds something in his hands. He raises it for her to take a look.

A doll.

It's dirt-smeared and soaked through. One button eye is missing, a tattered thread swinging in its place. Its yarn hair tangles in clumps, caked with mud and grime. "Look what I found."

"Where?"

"Just east of the creek bed. It's Emalie's, isn't it?"

Alara nods and crosses back through the water to meet him. She places her hand out. Auryn rests the doll in her palm. She inspects the dark stains, praying the copper splotches are anything other than what she believes them to be. "Take me there."

Auryn turns and she follows. Every tree seems to lean inwards as they move. Bark curls like listening ears. Their feet sink into soft earth, muffled by layers of wet leaves and mud. The path narrows, stretching deeper into the woods. Alara finds herself scanning the trees as they push forward, half expecting to catch a glimpse of icy blue eyes watching her from the shadows. She tries to push him from her thoughts, to no avail. He hadn't lunged—hadn't snarled... or hissed or done any of the things monsters usually do. He hadn't wished her dead. Yet—he smiled. Was he toying with her?

The stories rise unbidden—half whispered warnings from her mother. From the hunters before her. Before they all met the same fate. There are creatures in the woods that smile. Tricksters that wear skin like clothing. Beautiful but hollow. Things that don't bleed or stop for a conversation. They promise you lies, things you crave deeply. If you're dull enough to believe them...

He doesn't fit.

Her grip on the doll tightens. She replays the fight in her mind. How fast she'd moved. How hard she'd struck.

Had he made an offensive move?

She can't remember. He'd handed the blade over with ease, unbothered by her attempts to slay him. He'd laughed at her, amused and unthreatened. He had not come to harm her.

She opens her mouth and takes a deep breath, readying herself to confess to Auryn.

A scream splits through the trees. High. Shrill.

A child.

Alara locks eyes with Auryn before taking off in the direction of the desperate cry. Auryn darts after her just as fast. Branches snap at her face as she crashes through the undergrowth. The doll falls from her grasp, forgotten. Behind her Auryn curses, stumbling to keep up. The forest blurs to nothing but bark and shadows and the occasional branch to the cheek.

94

Another scream. Closer. More gut-wrenching than the last.

Alara vaults a fallen log, landing hard on the other side and hurls herself forward. Her heel slips in mud. She pushes off the earth and catches her footing. The trees are thicker and too close here. The ground rises and falls without warning. She slides down a shallow decline, grappling a sapling for balance before launching forward again. She can hear Auryn behind her, breathing harshly, boots slamming into the dirt. The ground rises fast. She stumbles uphill, hands skimming the earth as she claws her way to the top.

"Help me!"

Maren.

"Oh Gods—please help me!"

Alara crashes through a wall of brambles and bursts into a clearing. She stops there, unable to make sense of what she's seeing.

Maren sits on the ground, hovering over something. Her back faces them. She's breathing in spurts, her breath hitching repeatedly.

Off to the side, pressed against a moss-covered stone ridge, sits Emalie. The girl rocks gently. Her knees are drawn to her chest, thin arms wrapped tightly around them. She's hiding her face in her hands.

Auryn rushes to her side, dropping low to meet her. "It's alright," he says, soothingly. "You're safe now."

Emalie flinches but continues to rock. "She said we'd be safe if we didn't leave," she whispers, her voice broken and despaired.

Auryn wraps his arms around the girl and lifts her, carefully, holding her close. She buries her face in his chest, avoiding the sight of something.

Alara's eyes stay fixed on Maren. She watches her shoulders rise and fall too quickly. The sinking in her gut begins—slow, cold. "Maren..." Her voice is low, uncertain. "What is it?"

There's no answer. Just another shudder.

Alara steps forward and begins circling Maren, one foot at a time. She keeps moving, slowly, carefully.

Until she sees the body—small and still. And Maren's red-stained hands...

Isaac.

The boy, barely eleven, lies sprawled on his back beneath Maren. His tunic is soaked red at the collar. Alara gasps, noticing the spear lodged in his throat, poking out through the other side. Blood pools around his neck and upper torso. His body seems too small to hold so much blood. It continues to spill out of the wound.

Maren stays there, hands bloodied and trembling. Auryn focuses on her and squints his eyes. "Maren, what did you do?"

Chapter Ten

Alara falls to her knees the moment she sees him, her body giving out before her mind can catch up. "No. No..." She reaches out with a shaky hand and touches his face. Still warm. No rigor has taken hold. Had she been here minutes ago...

She pushes the thought from her mind. She presses two fingers to the side of the boy's neck. There's no flutter. No pulse. She slides a hand under his head, tilting it back slightly and presses to his chest, throwing her weight into desperate compressions. No use. Blood squirts out from the wound with each push. Alara stops and falls back, her hands sticky and warm.

She stumbles to her feet and staggers a few paces away, covering her mouth with a bloodied hand. She grips a tree branch, catching herself before retching into the earth. She heaves, over and over, trying to expel the remnants of everything she has just witnessed.

Isaac is dead. She was too late.

Her face twists and she wipes the bile from her mouth, blotching her lips red. She spits into the dirt and draws in a slow, shaky breath, preparing herself for what she must do next. The tremor in her hands fades as she straightens her back, breathing until she's steady enough to continue. Whatever had cracked in her, she covers it now. Unwilling to break.

She finally turns back to the scene. Maren remains still over the body. Auryn holds little Emalie tighter now, staring in disbelief. Alara moves to Maren's side. Her voice is cold and bitter when she speaks. "Did you do this?" No answer. "Maren! Did you do this?"

Maren nods her head once. So slight that Alara would have missed it if she wasn't studying her every move. Maren's eyes are still fixed on Isaac. At what she's done. She begins sobbing quietly, her body stuck in place. Her eyes unwilling to look away.

"Get up," Alara orders. Maren doesn't obey. "I said, get up!" She grabs Maren's upper arm and wrenches her to her feet, shoving her away from the body. Maren limps backwards from the force, tripping over herself and falling to the ground in defeat.

Alara returns her attention to Isaac, to the pike protruding from his neck. She needs to get it out. She needs to bring him back to Ravenforge. The shaft juts out from his throat, too heavy to stay upright. It leans to the side, exposing tissue and bone as it pulls.

Her hands hover over the wood, trembling just for a second. She inhales deeply and exhales just the same, before closing her hands around the shaft. She braces her foot against Isaac's chest. "I'm sorry," she says, her voice barely a whisper.

She tugs at the wood. The spear doesn't come willingly. It drags. The flesh resists. Skin and muscle give way with a slow sucking tension that makes her stomach turn again. She can feel every inch of the steel leaving his body.

When it comes free, she stumbles back, the weight of the spear suddenly too heavy in her hands. Blood drips from the tip, splattering her boot. Maren is watching her now. Alara returns her stare with all the poison and hate she can muster in a single look and throws the spear to the ground. It hits the dirt at Maren's feet with a thud.

"Tell me you deserve to be here now." Alara's voice rasps against the bile in her throat.

"Alara, we need to move," Auryn says, his voice quiet. He rocks the girl in his arms, trying to soothe her, trying to shield her from the bloody mess.

Maren looks back to Alara. There's no resistance in her eyes. No defiance. No possible defence. She looks at her with an expression Alara has never seen her wear.

Alara turns and crouches low, gathering Isaac in her arms. He's light. Thin. Fragile. Malnourished from four days alone in the woods. "Leave the spear," she says as she passes Maren. Her words force a small guttural breath from Maren's throat. She doesn't retrieve her weapon as she follows Alara and Auryn silently through the trees.

They get to the main path beneath the oak. A canopy of branches and leaves sway in the wind overhead, swishing and stirring as they move. Alara's eyes are locked on the path home. She holds Isaac tightly against her chest and quickens her pace. Maren falls behind, her limp forbidding her to keep up. The gap between them grows larger but still, she doesn't speak.

Isaac's body hangs from Alara's hands. One of his arms dangles from her clutch, swaying with each hurried step she takes. She keeps her gaze forward, her grip on the boy firm, and her boots steady on the forest floor. She doesn't look back. She refuses to look at the *protector* that drags behind. The title has become a curse—one akin to the bringer of tragedy.

Auryn walks beside Alara, Emalie cradled against him, keeping pace with ease. The girl's eyes are open but unfocused. Her fingers twitch now and then, a reminder of the blood that still flows through them.

Alara's mind spins as she tries to quiet it. She thinks of Alec. How will she explain that his friend won't be playing with him anymore? She thinks of Isaac's Mother. A widow, now alone. She had promised to bring him home.

Alara swallows hard against her foolishness. The air tastes of iron, seeping from the little body she carries.

Auryn exhales sharply and lifts his chin away from Emalie. "Bram!" he calls out to the forest. His voice is strong and booming. It pulls Alara back from her mind. "We have the children!" His words echo through the woods, bouncing between bark and leaves. He calls again, urging Bram to head home.

They push forward, Auryn repeating the same words as they go, praying it'll reach the right ears. As they enter the clearing Bram bounds through stinging nettle and low branches, stopping suddenly before them. He sees Auryn first, relief flooding his face at the sight of Emalie.

His eyes drift to Alara. The colour drains from his face. Isaac's body rests against her. He's painted with blood, the wound buried beneath it, hiding away the secrets of his death.

Bram doesn't speak. No one does. They walk slowly for the rest of the journey, only a few minutes out from Ravenforge now. They drag their feet. Maren manages to catch up but remains intentionally behind the group.

Alara stops before the fence, dreading the moments to come. Auryn moves on, through the fields, cradling Emalie all the while. Bram walks at his side. Maren trudges behind them, head down, her limp much more visible since the incident.

The first voice rises, a woman at the far edge of the field, near the cottages. She cups her hands around her mouth and calls out, alerting whoever is listening. Her words don't carry clearly but heads turn and people emerge from their homes. Villagers gather, huddling with anticipation of the hunters' approach.

Alara takes a shuddery breath and wills her legs to move forward. There's nothing left to do now but bring Isaac home. Alec's voice plays in her head, soft and sombre.

At least you can bring their bodies home for their parents.

They see Emalie first—silent and still in Auryn's embrace. Someone cries out, loud enough for the whole village to hear. "She's alive!"

Alara's breath catches as she sees Alec run out from Deia's home, berry juice stains on his face. He comes running down the dirt path and into the fields, calling for Emalie and Isaac, wearing the biggest grin Alara has ever seen. Deia trails behind him, wiping her hands on her apron. Alec keeps running, until his eyes meet Alara and drop down to the weight she holds in her arms.

Isaac's body swings with each move Alara makes. Alec's mouth opens but nothing comes out.

The joy leaves his body like a flame snuffed out. Deia sees too. She gasps and covers her mouth with a floury hand.

A scream rips through the air. It doesn't sound human. It's raw and ragged, rising from somewhere guttural. It punches through Alara like a blade. The sound rattles the village, causing everyone to halt and stare.

Isaac's mother comes barrelling into the field, barefoot and wild-eyed. She runs towards them, her skirt twisting around her ankles, threatening to trip her. She continues to scream. It breaks and claws its way out of her throat again and again as she sprints to them. "Isaac!" Her voice cracks so violently it sounds as though it should tear her in half. She approaches Alara and takes her son from her arms. Together, they fall to the ground. She scoops him onto her lap, fighting through the desperate wails that refuse to stay hidden behind her lips. Her hands fly over his body, his arms, his face—searching for any sign of life. "My sweet boy," she chokes out, pulling him to her, rocking him. "My baby boy..." She continues to weep as she sways, trying desperately to soothe something that can no longer be comforted. She pulls him close to her chest, nuzzling her face into his blood-streaked hair.

Alara stays there, frozen, watching, until she breathes, "I'm so sorry." Isaac's mother doesn't answer. She doesn't look away from her boy, unable to hear the words through her broken sobs.

Her cries boom through Alara's head. She clutches at her skull, silently begging for the pain to stop and looks around at the faces of the villagers. All eyes are on Isaac and Melinda. Many of them cry alongside her. Others wear mixed expressions of fear, shock, disgust. Maren is not amongst them. She has disappeared altogether.

Alara steps back, tearing herself away from the scene. She marches off through the field, intent on justice.

She passes Alec and Deia. Her brother refuses to meet her eyes. "Deia, bring him inside," she says. Deia nods and places a hand on Alec's back, turning him towards her cottage.

Emalie's mother and father rush past Alara towards Auryn, shouting for their girl in disbelief.

Alara doesn't watch the reunion. Her mind is locked on locating Maren. Isaac's mother's screams still ring in her ears, even with the distance between them. Her arms feel hollow now, having gotten used to the weight of him. Her hands twitch at her sides, her fingers curling in on themselves. She walks down the main path, scanning for the woman that ended the life of someone so innocent, so undeserving of the fate that was forced upon him. She's nowhere to be found.

Coward.

She keeps moving, past the cottages, past the old chapel, and the market. She passes the barracks where she used to train relentlessly, refusing to stop her search. Refusing to let Maren get away with this.

Bram calls out to her. He chases after her as she continues her mission. "Where are you going? They want an explanation."

Alara doesn't stop. "That's exactly what I intend to give them. Where's Maren? Did you see where she went?"

He falls in stride with her and points to the far fences. "I think I saw her go that way."

Alara turns down the path. One less travelled in the village. It leads to nothing but dead soil and fence.

Finally, she spots her, curled up beside a rotting birch. She rushes towards her, fury in every step she takes. "You coward!" The words make Maren jump. She turns to them, face streaked with tears, hands smudged with blood. "You killed him and you run?"

Bram inhales sharply. "She did what?"

"Her spear killed Isaac. I pulled it from his throat." Alara storms over to where Maren sits slumped against the gnarled roots of the dying birch, head bowed as though she's trying to disappear. She grabs Maren by the front of her shirt and yanks her upright. "What do you have to say for yourself?" she shouts, her voice raw with rage. Maren is silent. She stares at the ground, refusing to meet her eyes. "Look at me!" Alara's grip tightens and her fists slam into the trunk just inches from Maren's head. The bark cracks under her knuckles. Maren flinches but still refuses to look up. "Speak!" she demands, as though she's commanding a disobedient hound too slow to learn a simple trick.

"They'll burn her for this," Bram says, cutting through the tension with his statement.

Alara's eyes stay locked on Maren, her lips curving downwards. "Maybe they should," she says flatly.

Maren just stands there, leaning against the trunk of the tree. Her eyes remain fixed on the ground like she's hoping to vanish into it.

Bram steps in, voice low but firm. "I don't know what happened out there... but we need to decide what comes next." He looks between the two. "Did Auryn see?"

Alara's gaze hasn't left Maren, hasn't even flickered. She nods, slowly.

Bram sighs. "Then we need to find him."

Alara continues to stare at Maren. Always desperate to prove herself. Always proving useless.

She stares and all she can see is Isaac.

The shredded flesh pulling away from him with the tug of Maren's spear.

The blood drying in his yellow hair.

The look on Alec's face when he saw him. How she had failed him. *Again.*

Her hand drifts to her side, fingers brushing the worn leather of the sheath. The dagger is there. Always is. She could draw it in a blink. She could press it to Maren's throat and drag it across with one clean pull. She could end this. It would be so easy. No council. No talk. No trial. Just silence and blood. How things always end.

So easy.

She breathes against her thoughts. The fire dims, not with mercy but exhaustion. Her fingers fall away from the sheath. "You do what you must," she mutters. Her voice remains flat, empty. She turns without waiting for a response, leaving Maren behind. "I need a drink."

Chapter Eleven

Alara pushes open the heavy wooden door to the tavern, the golden light flooding over her as she enters. Inside, it's dim and warm, the kind of soft amber that eases the eyes and slows the pulse. Candlelight flickers low in iron sconces, painting the structural beams in subtle shades of orange.

Two of the tavern's regulars sit slouched at the end of the bar top, heads low over their drinks. They glance at the door when it creaks open, then quickly turn away from the sight of her.

The bartender, Benjamin, stands behind the bar, wiping the counter with a rag that could use a good wash. He's stout and thick-armed, his dark brows knitted together beneath the glint of his balding scalp. His curled moustache twitches slightly as she steps inside. His hand stills. "Alara," he says, not surprised, just bracing. She only comes when something awful has happened.

"Ben," she replies, dryly.

Risa is stacking mugs in the corner, counting each one out loud as she piles them. She's shorter than Alara—somehow—and built like a flame—small, bright, and dangerous when provoked. She throws a grin over her shoulder as Alara brushes by.

"Rough night?" Benjamin calls out.

She doesn't reply. She walks behind the bar without ask and reaches for a dark glass bottle near the back of the display. The liquid inside gleams molasses brown in the firelight. Not whiskey, not quite but close enough. It's strong, burns going down, and nobody ever asks what's in it. She yanks the cork loose with her teeth, spitting it into the sink and takes a deep pull. The heat spreads down her throat and hits her empty belly, settling there like coals. She turns to leave.

Before she reaches the door Benjamin calls out, "I guess I'll add that to your tab."

She grimaces at the bartender, so full of dreams about owning a tavern somewhere far from Ravenforge. A place where people still smile. Where coin passes hand for drink. He speaks of other places as if they're real. As if they aren't just scraps of rumours passed down by those too stubborn to accept the truth—Ravenforge is the last village still standing.

She turns halfway, catching Risa's crooked grin and lifts the bottle in the air. A mock toast. "To this whole fucking day," she says, taking another swig off the bottle. The door swings shut behind her.

Alara notices a few villagers heading her way down the main path by the chapel. She stops short and turns behind the tavern, hopping the fence.

No more people. Not now.

By the time her bottle is half-empty, her legs have gone numb. She stumbles deeper into the trees, the warmth and noise of Ravenforge long since swallowed by the forest.

It doesn't welcome her. It never does. Damp earth sucks at her boots. Branches snag her hair, like fingers trying to hold her back. An owl hoots from the darkness, low and mournful.

The bottle swings from Alara's hand, half-forgotten now. She squeezes her eyes shut against the events of the day.

It starts with the council meeting, the betrayal of her own people. Haven't they learnt anything? Tilda's final words. Elowen's averted gaze. Thomas's smug, prideful smile when he gets his way. The old council is just that. Old. Stuck in their ways, though their ways prove to bring nothing but power and ignorance. She rolls her eyes at them, though none are present and takes another drink from the bottle.

Serilda's voice comes next. *The girl should not go.* Why must she always speak in riddles? In half-conversations, finished only within the confines of her mind. Why can't she be direct? To the point.

She scoffs and puts the bottle to her lips again, welcoming the tingle down her throat. Her stomach has gotten used to the poison now. She sways, blinking madly at the teetering trees. Her knuckles whiten around the neck of the bottle. She tips it again.

Isaac comes to her next. The spear buried so deeply into his neck. Her two hands gripped tightly around the base and the strength she'd used to pull it free. The way it dragged from his throat, refusing to let go of the child. Alec running into the field, the biggest smile plastered across his purple-stained face. The look in his eyes when he noticed the body. She hears Isaac's mother. Screaming. Ripping at her own vocal cords from the strain. How she held him and whispered into his bloody hair.

She leans forward, her stomach twisting now. She heaves but nothing comes up. Only fire in her throat.

She closes her eyes and Maren appears. Her blade throbs against her hip. She'd come so close to drawing her dagger. She'd wanted to. Just a flick of the wrist across her thin throat and it would've all been—

She lurches against a tree, breathing hard and presses her forehead into the bark. She turns, sinking down to the roots. Everything spins and swells. Her head drops back against the trunk.

She closes her eyes again and a different pair stare back at her. Icy blue. The stranger with the pale, wind-swept hair. She watches the sunlight catch it as he flashes that same barely-amused smirk across his lips. He moves too fluid, too gentle. Like he's humouring her.

Her eyes open and she blinks sluggishly into the dark. "Hey!" she calls, voice thick. She pushes herself up from the roots, the bottle still swinging lazily at her side. "Fuckhead! You still watching me?"

Clacking teeth answer her call. She spins fast and out of the dark it emerges. Sharp, thin teeth glint in the moonlight, long limbs twitching. NeedleTeeth. It crawls towards her.

"Oh," Alara says, tilting her head. "Watch this asshole!"

She surges forward, too fast for her balance and slices clumsily. The blade grazes the beast's arm. It shrieks and bats her away like a fly. She hits a tree with a crack, the bottle smashing from the force. She slumps to the ground, air punched from her lungs. She tries to stand but stumbles over.

She laughs. "Guess this is it, huh?" Her voice is hoarse, almost fond, welcoming the end. She closes her eyes as the monster creeps closer, rattling its teeth at her. With her eyes closed, Alara sees Alec reaching out for her. Her face tightens, the laughter catching in her throat. "I'm sorry, mama," she mumbles, bracing for her fate.

Something hits the creature—hard. The sound it makes isn't a shriek but a wet gurgling scream. She opens her eyes. The stranger is crouched over the beast, tearing into it—with his teeth. Dark blood sprays out of its neck. The NeedleTeeth thrashes and falls still. The stranger rises, spitting something dark onto the roots beside her.

Alara stares, stunned. Then she starts to laugh. "Did you just bite that thing?" She laughs harder, tipping sideways. "That's disgusting!"

He strides towards her, plucking her fallen dagger from the ground. He crouches to her level. "Are you drunk?"

"Yep," she beams. "Now, are you going to tell me who you are, or am I going to have to kick your ass again?"

He blinks and looks her over. She's utterly dishevelled. There's blood on her cheek and leaves in her hair. He lets out a dry scoff. "Kick *my* ass?"

"I'll do it!" She lifts a finger and waggles it in a vaguely threatening way.

He raises an eyebrow. "You can barely stand." He hands over the blade. She takes it, reluctantly, having forgotten she'd even lost it.

She squints at him. "Are you a hunter?"

Offense crosses his face. "No, Alara. I'm not a hunter."

"Fae?" she presses, squinting harder.

"No."

She leans in closer. "You're not a Scab, are you?" She reaches out and starts poking at his face and torso.

He exhales sharply. "What are you doing?" he says, pulling away.

"Looking. Don't get shy *now*," she snorts.

"You shouldn't be out here. You're hammered."

"I'm fine." She pushes herself upright and immediately stumbles. He catches her under the arms, annoyed and amused all at once. She leans into him with a sigh. "I miss my bottle."

"I think you've had plenty," he scolds her. "What are you doing out here like this*?*"

"I asked my question first." She pushes off him, regaining a small amount of balance and stands on her own. "Actually, I have a better one. Why are you following me?"

He looks her over again before answering with a shrug. "I guess I'm bored."

Her face twists with judgment. "You stalk people when you're bored?"

"I heard you humming out here a few nights ago. You were humming and killing. It was strange."

"That's me. Alara the freak. The girl who sings to her mother's corpse and the girl who makes friends with rotting Scabs. Pleased to meet you." She narrows her eyes at him. "Now, who the hell are *you*?"

"You can call me Jax."

Alara chortles. "That's a stupid name." She wobbles slightly and catches herself on a low branch. "Well, Jax, I've never seen anyone kill something with their teeth before."

"I didn't kill it," he says in a matter-of-fact tone. "It should be waking up soon."

Before she can make sense of the confession, the chittering resumes. Slow and quiet at first, then sharper. Faster. The familiar sick clicking rises from behind her, growing louder by the second.

She turns to see the NeedleTeeth twitching in place, its limbs spasming, jerking and demented—like a marionette whose strings are being pulled by the puppeteer of Hell. Its balance is off. It sways slightly. Its head lolls to the side for a moment, before snapping upright, locking its black eyes on Alara.

She takes a step back. "Why didn't you kill it?"

Jax smiles smugly. "I thought you wanted me to watch *you* kill it." He winks at her and, with an exaggerated gesture, steps back a few paces and sweeps his arms wide, presenting her the forest floor. "I'm watching."

Alara curses under her breath just as the creature lunges for her. She pivots to move but the ground is uneven and in her intoxicated state she falls, tripping over a protruding root. She crashes down hard, narrowly missing the monster's claws. It rakes the tree behind her.

Jax clicks his tongue. "Sloppy."

"Fuck you," she snarls, scrambling onto her elbows.

The NeedleTeeth jumps on top of her in an instant, its full weight pressing her down. She turns beneath it and holds it back with her arm, straining as her vision swims with liquor. Its jaws snap too close to her face. Hot, acidic drool drips from its mouth, spilling onto her neck. She screams and reaches for her dagger, scrambling to unsheathe it. More drool hits the side of her face. She lets out a battle cry, finally getting her blade free and drives it into the creature's neck. Leaning into it, she pushes down until the steel reaches the chest cavity. The NeedleTeeth slumps on top of her. The green runes make her eyes pulse and her head throb. She pushes the beast off her with a grunt and stumbles to her feet.

Jax steps closer to where she stands, clapping slowly. A round of applause. "What a kill," he says, chuckling to himself, like he'd just placed a bet on her life.

Alara begins to regain her wit. She storms over to Jax, refusing to be made a spectacle of and slams her fist square into his cocky smile. His head turns from the hit. He laughs and wipes his bottom lip with his thumb. She raises her blade to him, remembering this man is no friend of hers.

He sighs. "Oh, come on, this again?"

She glares through her double vision. "You almost got me killed!"

He shakes his head. "You almost got yourself killed the moment you stepped into these woods with that bottle in your hand." He takes a step closer to her. "*I* saved your life," he says, tilting his head to the side. "Technically."

"You left it alive and waited for it to come after me!"

"And you're *fine*," he says, unbothered. "Not to mention lucky that *I* found you and not one of the others."

"The others? The other *what?*"

He laughs again. "I'm not spilling my secrets to a girl that doesn't trust me."

"Why would I trust you? I don't know you. Or what you are. And you just used me as some sick form of entertainment!"

He rolls his shoulders in annoyance. "You're *so* emotional."

"Get away from me," she hisses through clenched teeth, still holding her dagger between them.

He straightens his posture slightly, seemingly debating if he wants to go a round with the liquored huntress but drops his shoulders, deciding against it. He holds his hands up, palms first, "As you wish," and vanishes into the trees, the forest closing around him without a thought.

Alara stands alone in the dark, breathing deeply, trying to connect herself with her body through the haze of alcohol. She keeps her blade in hand, refusing to drop her guard now. She closes her eyes and tries to steady herself. Her body returns to her in pieces.

First, the heavy weight of her legs. Next, the sting from the acid on her neck and along her cheek bone. She winces against the sharp pain. And finally, the cold air and damp clothes she wears. The wind swirls around her making her shiver as it slithers through her wet, red-stained shirt. She presses a hand to the tree in front of her, grounding herself to the rough bark.

Another breath. Less shaky than the ones before. Calmer. The world begins to sharpen. Crickets chirp faintly nearby. The wind tugs on her clothes again.

Inhale. Exhale.

She opens her eyes and scans the trees where he stood, moments before, searching for any flicker of movement, for the glint of those piercing blue eyes beneath the leaves. All she sees are shadows made of branches and greenery.

She lets out a long, exasperated breath through pursed lips and pushes off the tree, regaining her balance through the adrenaline.

She turns and starts walking the path back to Ravenforge, her boots heavier than usual. She forces herself to continue, though her body aches for rest. Occasionally, she glances behind her, watching for those blue eyes she can't seem to shake from her head.

Chapter Twelve

Alec shakes my shoulder.

"Alara, wake up!" he whispers with breathless excitement. He shakes me again. "Come on, you have to see."

I open my eyes to find Alec's face, just inches from mine. His smile stretches to his cheeks. His eyes are dancing as he bounces on the balls of his feet.

"Farmer Davit said Isaac and I can ride one of the horses!"

He grabs my hand, tugging me upright, dragging me to the door with enthusiasm. I follow. My head throbs beneath the morning sun, a dull ache that burns behind my eyes. The light is too warm, too golden. The village hums as we cross the field.

Alec runs ahead, barefoot in the grass, waving both arms above his head. "Sir Davit! I brought her!"

Two figures stand in the field, backs turned. Farmer Davit and—Isaac? The old work horse pulls a cart slowly behind them near the edge of the field.

They don't move. Not at Alec's voice. Not at the sound of our steps. Not even when the wind shifts the tall stalks and they smack them in the face.

I stop walking. A quiet itch creeps up the back of my neck. They're too still. Their shoulders don't rise with breath. Not a twitch. Not a stir.

Alec goes silent beside me. When I glance at him, he's no longer bouncing on his heels. He stands stiffly, staring straight ahead. His grin hasn't faded. It's only stretched. Too wide. Too many teeth.

My stomach knots. Something is wrong. My body knows it before my mind catches up. I take a step back.

The figures in the field turn in unison towards me. Farmer Davit's face matches Alec's—stretched, unnatural. Isaac's eyes are pale and clouded. Maren's spear protrudes from his throat. Blood spills down his chest, soaking the wheat around him. A buzzing builds in my ears.

That's not Alec.
That's not Isaac.
None of this is mine.

I turn to run but collide with something solid.

Someone.

I fall back into the grass, scrambling to my knees, trying to push myself up with my hands. My body weighs more than I can bear. I look up.

"Mama?"

She stands over me. Her hair hangs in knots over her shoulders. Dried blood clings to her chest. Her jaw sags loosely open. Above it, her eyes are missing, the sockets dark and hollow. She opens her mouth. But it isn't her voice that comes out. It's Isaac's mother's. She screams, raw and brutal, the wail of her soul tearing in half. It shreds through me. I drop to my knees, clutching my head. The screaming doesn't stop, doesn't waiver. It burns my skull. Blood trickles from my ears, hot and wet, soaking my palms as I try to cover them. I shriek from the pain but I don't hear myself. My cry blends into the keening scream surrounding me. It overtakes the field as it flees my mother's lips.

And still—beneath the shrieking and ringing—a voice begins to rise, deep at the back of my head. Low, familiar. Too calm for the chaos erupting around me.

The blood sings.

I turn, hands still clamped to my ears, fingers sticky with blood.

Across the field, the grass begins to split. It separates, as though the earth is exhaling a secret

it has been choking on. Its silhouette pushes upwards from the soil—slow and deliberate.
It's towering over me now. Over the field. Over the imposters beside me. A shadow, pitch black. Its arms hang too long at its sides. Its fingers brush the wheat as it climbs. Antlers twist upwards from its head, jagged and gnarled, cracking the sky above it. The scream fades behind me but the voice remains. Like a promise carved in stone.

The blood...

It moves forward, the ground withering beneath each step.

Is mine.

"Alara?"

Alara stirs, grumbling against the strips of sunlight shining down on her through the tattered curtains above.

Something small and soft shakes her shoulder. She opens her eyes slowly, squinting against the pressure in her head. "Alec?"

He stands at the edge of her bed, rocking slightly, hesitant to wake her.

Alara lifts the blanket, offering him the chance to get under.

He shakes his head. "You should wake up. You missed the council meeting. And you're filthy."

She's lying on her back, the usual bunching in her mattress digging into her spine. She raises her hands out, placing them before her face and squeezing her eyes, willing them to adjust. Her hands sway in front of her, though she holds them perfectly still. Even through the rippling in her vision she can see the skin is dark and stained.

"Alec... I must've—"

"You passed out."

"Right..." She turns her head to him, slowly, against the splitting ache in her temple. She focuses on his little features. The sight of her little brother sobers her faster than any cold river ever could.

His cheeks are puffy, the skin beneath his eyes swollen and bruised from sleeplessness. His lashes are stuck together in clumps. His lips are pale, his expression jaded with the kind of grief that drags years behind it. He stares at Alara with a faraway look she doesn't recognize.

"Maren didn't go to the meeting either. Everyone is mad," he mutters. "And no one saw Isaac's mama." His voice breaks on his friend's name. The sound of it splinters something in her.

She sits up slowly, fighting the stabbing behind her eyes and reaches for him. Alec jerks away. He turns his back on her and crouches beside the hearth. He starts scribbling something furiously on loose parchment.

"Alec..." her voice comes out hoarse, dry. "I'm so sorry..."

"Just leave me alone, Alara. Okay?" His voice snaps through the still cottage, too sharp for someone his age. "*They* need you more than I do."

He turns back to his parchment. The humming he usually makes when he draws is absent. There's no lightness in his movements. Just hard frantic scribbling.

She watches him work in silence, peeking over his shoulder to get a glimpse. The sketch is a blur of dark strokes, messy, yet deliberate. A black shape smeared so deeply it warps the paper. At the top of the void, two jagged antlers rise from the shadow. Her stomach sinks.

"Where have you seen that?" she asks, her voice barely audible.

He doesn't look up. "I had a nightmare," he murmurs, dragging the charcoal back over the page, pressing harder until the center becomes a solid black pit. She watches the shape spread, watches him bury it in shadow like something that should not be seen. "Deia said I can stay with her for a little while." The statement cuts Alara deep. Alec lightens his tone, noticing the harshness to his voice. "If that's okay..." he adds.

She clears her throat before she speaks, combating the lump at the back of it. "Yeah... that's fine," she breathes. A lie. She pushes herself out of bed, every movement slow and deliberate. She walks over to Alec and presses a kiss to the top of his head. He doesn't react, doesn't lean into it like he normally would.

She drags her feet over to the cracked mirror propped up on the wall. One look at her jagged reflection confirms last night wasn't all a nightmare. Raw stains trail along her cheek and neck, blooming in angry red patches. She looks pale. Hollow. Her face sinks in along her eyes and cheekbones. Her lips are cracked. She can't remember the last time she ate or drank from anything aside from yesterday's bottle. Alara cups cold water from the basin and splashes it on her face. It stings where the burns catch it. She flinches.

The water in the wash basin is cloudy. Murky with dirt and blood. It needs to be changed. She turns away from it to reach for the pale-green jar on the shelf beneath the broken mirror. She dabs the ointment to the acid scars, wincing as it stings, then settles. Her clothes are stiff with dried blood, the fabric crusted and tight across her shoulders. She peels it off and finds a fresh tunic to slip on, tucking it into the top of her trousers.

With one last glance at Alec, she steps outside and heads towards Deia's cottage. The promise of warmth and bread pulls her like a lifeline.

The stew is cold but Alara shovels it down like it's the first thing she's eaten in days—because it is. She tears into a half loaf of bread with her teeth. Crumbs scatter down her shirt as she scoops the last bit of broth from the wooden bowl.

"Sorry there's no more. The boy got here before you," Deia says calmly. Alara doesn't mind. It eases her to know Alec is being looked after. He eats like a starved little wolf and always leaves just enough behind to make you feel guilty taking the rest.

She swallows hard, the last bit of stew fighting to stay down. "What's the meat?"

"Rabbit," Deia says, already elbow deep in another batch of dough on the table.

That explains the texture.

Alara doesn't comment. She is too hungry to care. She shoves the last of the loaf in her mouth, barely chewing it and chases it with a mug of warm water. Her stomach gurgles in gratitude. She wipes her face on her sleeve and leans back in her chair. Her voice comes out quieter than she means it to. "Alec will be staying with you for a while?"

Deia doesn't look up from her work. "Yes. I told him that's fine by me. Besides..." her voice softens, almost fondly. "I think the boy needs a mother type right now."

Alara stills. The words hit somewhere sore. She nods faintly, her eyes dropping to her hands. "I'm not really... that. I try but..." Her voice falters and she lets it drop, the ache in her throat tightening. "I did my best, Deia," she says after a long pause. Her voice is small, defeated. "I got there too late..."

Deia steps away from the table and rests a floury hand on Alara's back. Her palm is warm. She rubs her hand in small circles. "I know, child."

Alara holds her breath, composing herself before speaking. "Alec hates me."

"Watch your tongue." Deia's voice sharpens a little. "That boy doesn't have a hateful bone in his body. He just needs time. He's grieving. He needs a warm bed and a belly full of sweets."

Alara nods and a small smile tugs at her lips. "Thank you," she says quietly. "For everything. I don't know what we'd do without you."

Deia waves her off and returns to her dough. "Oh, hush. You'd manage just fine without me. But it's easier when someone's got a full stomach, hmm?"

Alara smiles at her with all she has left to offer.

"I'll take good care of the boy, yeah? You focus on getting your head right."

Alara lifts herself from the chair. She wraps her arms around Deia. A silent thank you. Deia places a hand on Alara's arm around her neck and pats it gently.

"Don't you have somewhere to be, child?" Alara releases her and steps away. The warmth of the embrace fades quickly. She steps towards the door and slowly exhales, soaking up every bit of quiet she can before she has to face the world outside.

The moment she swings the door open a voice cuts across the lane.

"Alara!" Auryn's tall frame rounds the corner at a jog, his long strides closing the distance too fast. Bram is close behind him, his hair unkempt, sleeves rolled up to the elbows like he's been working—or arguing.

Her boots hit the dirt hard, stride steady, jaw set.

"Alara, wait—"

She doesn't. Her shoulders don't even twitch as they call her name. Her steps are even, deliberate. She keeps moving, even as the two hunters fall in step beside her. There's a flatness to her. Something locked down tight behind her eyes.

"We told them we didn't see what happened to Isaac," Auryn says, keeping his voice low, sheltered from listening ears. "Maren's shut herself in. And Emalie hasn't spoken since the forest."

Alara doesn't answer. Her boots press into the narrow, overgrown path that cuts behind the market. Her pace never shifts. The brambles claw at her legs, snagging on the worn leather of her trousers but she refuses to let them slow her down.

Auryn and Bram share a glance before following her in.

"Alara..." Bram tries, his breath catching as some rogue brambles attempt to tie him up. "Where are you going?"

The tall weeds thin out as Serilda's crooked little cottage appears ahead, slouched into the hill, the earth slowly digesting it through the years.

Auryn catches her arm as she reaches the warped door. "We need to deal with this," he whispers, eyes darting to the glowing windows of the worn cottage.

Alara turns, calmly. Too calm. Too still for the thoughts running wild in her head. Her voice is level. "This is not on me. Or you." Auryn drops his grip on her. She looks between the two. "This is on the council. They put Maren back in those woods. Isaac's blood is on their hands."

She doesn't stay for a conversation. The wood groans softly as she steps inside the oddly lit room. Without looking back, she slips inside, shutting the door behind her.

"My girl," Serilda's voice bounces off the walls, giddy and childlike. "You've come to visit!" The air is thick with the scent of dried flowers and herbs. Serilda sits cross-legged in the center of a circle of petals and twigs. A single unlit candle sits at her knees. Her fingers hover above it, twitching slightly, following something only she can sense.

Alara raises an eyebrow. "What are you doing?"

"Shhh!" Serilda lifts her hand without looking at her. "I'm listening to the trees."

Alara glances around the cottage. "You're inside, Auntie."

Serilda turns her head and smiles, nodding as if Alara's just confirmed something.

Alara sighs. She doesn't have the energy for this today. Her body still aches from her night of drink, her head still pounding. But there's something about the flicker of peace on Serilda's face that draws her forward anyway. She sinks to the floor across from her and folds her legs—mimicking the way Serilda sits.

"Are you going to light the wick?"

"Oh, yes." Serilda moves her hand, gliding her palm above the candle. A spark leaps into being the moment her skin passes over the wick. There's a soft pop as the flame ignites, curling upwards in a gentle coil.

Alara chuckles involuntarily under her breath.

"You've always loved that, Lyssa."

Alara stiffens at her mother's name. "I'm Alara," she says sharply.

There's no apology in Serilda's expression, only a strange softness. "Yes, I know who you are."

Silence settles between them. The candle's flame dances from side to side, disturbed by wind that isn't present. Serilda closes her eyes. Alara watches her. The way her lashes flutter, the way her fingers continue to twitch, as though something unseen is crawling along her skin.

Alara finally breaks the silence. "Did you know what would happen to Isaac?"

Serilda's eyes open. Hurt flashes through them, like lightning under water. "No, my girl. I did not know."

Alara breathes unevenly. "Then why did you come to the meeting? You told me Maren shouldn't go back out."

Serilda gives a slow shake of her head. "No. The trees told you that." She gestures faintly at the walls. "They speak in fractured voices. They do not show me what is to come, only what has already happened."

"What does that even mean..." Alara mutters, rubbing at her temples.

Serilda flashes her that smile again. The same sweet, faraway thing she does during the worst possible moments.

She had smiled just like that at Lyssa's funeral, amongst a crowd of puffy eyes and shattered hope. She had smiled just like that when the bakery burned down and Deia was beside herself over it. It never fits the moment and yet always remains on her face.

"A child is dead, Serilda. I don't have the patience for this."

"Patience is everything," Serilda replies, folding her hands in her lap. "How do we hear the answers if we do not wait in the silence?"

Alara closes her eyes and draws in a long breath through her nose, holding it in her chest until her ribs ache. She exhales slowly, steady, like she's trying to expel embers threatening to catch on fire.

Fine. I'll play along.

"I want to ask you something... About my dreams," she says, rubbing her hands together, not quite sure how to explain herself. "Nightmares, really. They're always nightmares."

Serilda's spine straightens. Her eyes light up with an excitement most people reserve for festivals and birthdays. "Go on."

"There's something I keep seeing in them," Alara continues. "A shadow with antlers. I never get a good look at it. I can never see its face. Alec was drawing it this morning. But that's not possible..." She shakes her head. "I don't know what it means..."

"You will," Serilda says with quiet certainty. "When the time comes." Her smile dims. "It has already happened."

Alara's throat tightens. "And Alec?"

Serilda's gaze drifts to the candle flickering between them. Her expression softens, her smile slipping away. Her lips move but she's not speaking to Alara. Words begin to tumble out in a whisper, almost too fast to catch. Alara leans in.

"Blood at the threshold. Bones in the wheat. Ashes and fire at the doors. When he comes..."

Alara's brow furrows. "Serilda..."

Serilda keeps chanting, muttering to no one. "Too late. Too late. The roots drink deep. The witch... speaks her final word without a head to wear it."

"Serilda." Alara snaps two fingers in front of her face. The crack pulls Serilda back. She smiles at her again. Alara groans. "Can we please get through this conversation without you talking to yourself?"

Serilda tips her head up slightly, giving Alara the attention she begs for. "My girl..." she says, almost mournfully. "I'm speaking to whomever will listen. No one ever listens..."

Chapter Thirteen

The clearing behind the chapel is quiet. No birds sing. No breeze stirs. The forest itself has gone still with the rest of the mourning village.

The ground has been swept clean. Isaac's body rests on a wooden slab, wrapped in white linen stained with lavender and juniper oils. His face remains outside the fabrics. His skin is too pale to belong to the living. Elder Tilda holds a lit bundle of sage in her hand. She twirls it where he lies, the smoke drifting upwards.

Melinda—Isaac's mother, sits closest to him at the base of the slab, knees tucked, hands folded tightly in her lap. She hasn't moved since dawn. She watches her son with vacant eyes and hollow cheeks. Whatever tears she has shed have long since dried. She stares on, her mind somewhere else entirely.

The hunters form a line to the left. Auryn, Bram, and Alara stand tall with straight backs, dressed in full gear—leather, iron, and dull blades to show respect. Jorin stands beside them, learning the weight of his path too soon amongst the others. Maren is not present. Refusing to leave her home, even to pay the respect she owes to her fallen brother. Alara stands near the slab, her chest straining as she keeps her eyes forward. She cannot break now, not when the village is watching, not when Alec is still looking through her like a stranger.

Surrounding the scene, villagers gather in solemn silence. Some clutch their children, others hold themselves, watching with tired sadness. Deia lingers towards the back, her palms steady on Alec's shoulders. He doesn't glance in Alara's direction. Not once. He holds little Emalie's hand firmly, her eyes fixed on the ground. Her parents stand at her side, watching her more than they look ahead, refusing to let her out of their sight for even a moment since her return.

A bell tolls once, low and long. Its echoes spread to the trees. Elder Tilda steps forward. Her cloak trails over the dirt as she moves slowly to the center where the slab lies. In her hands she carries a small bowl of fine charcoal. She dips her thumb in it and presses a mark to Isaac's forehead—a spiral nested in the sun, Ravenforge's ancient symbol. A guide for the soul.

"May the Gods accept this young warrior, taken too soon from the fields of battle, into their kingdom." Her voice is loud and steady. Authority ringing out into the crowd of her people. "May he find no fear in the road ahead. No pain in his crossing." She sets down the bowl and replaces it with a skinny clay vessel, its rim stained with gold. Elder Thomas reaches her side and guides Isaac's mouth open. Tilda tips the vase. Honey catches firelight. Thick, slow-moving, and sacred. "Accept our offering on the tongue." She tips the jar higher, pouring the remaining contents into Isaac's parted lips. "Welcome him with his kin who have fallen before he."

Alec turns his face away, eyes clenched shut. He drops Emalie's hand. Deia wraps her arms around him, pulling him into her chest. Alara watches, her throat burning. She wants nothing more than to gather him in her arms and tell him it's over. That he's safe. That she's sorry... But she doesn't move from her duty.

Tilda reaches for a pouch next, casting a handful of dried blueberries into the ceremonial fire at her side. Flames crackle as they hit, spitting up smoke in curling threads of violet and grey.

"Protect him from the ones that steal," she continues. "Let no dark touch his bones. Let no hunger smell his soul."

Alara watches the crowd. She looks into the familiar faces around her, her heart tearing at their agony. A hunter down. A promise destroyed.

Auryn rests a hand on Alara's shoulder. The contact is light, yet solid. She stiffens at first, not expecting the comfort but doesn't pull away from it.

The smoke from the iron basin continues to curl upwards, thin and silver as the berries burn away, reaching towards a sky that offers no sign of listening.

A tremor passes through the crowd, so subtle it's almost imagined. But when the people begin to shift and avert their eyes, the presence is clear.

Serilda stands just beyond the firelight. No one sees her arrive. She appears as if summoned by the offering itself. She doesn't speak. Her long hair hangs loose and matted, threads of ribbon tangled through the strands. Her bare feet are smeared with mud and grass. She looks as though she has been plucked from a different time. As though she shouldn't be here and yet she always is. She doesn't approach. She doesn't offer a prayer. She stands there. Watching. She lifts her head slightly, the corners of her mouth twitching, willing her usual mutterings to stay safely behind the trembling of her teeth.

Elder Tilda notices the shift in her people but continues the ritual with perfect composure.

She turns her gaze to the hunters, signalling them to begin.

Alara steps forward with Bram and Auryn at her side. What comes next is unspoken but understood. The three of them move in practiced unison, each placing a hand beneath the wooden frame. It creaks faintly as they lift it from the ground—slowly, carefully, keeping Isaac level as the linen moves against the slab.

Jorin watches from the line. His eyes are wide, his fists tight. He follows them as they walk on.

They reach the back door to the chapel, half-hidden behind a wall of vines and brambles. Auryn opens it without a word. The air changes as they step inside. It's warm and stale with a moistness to it.

The stairwell leading down is steep and carved into the earth with precision. The warriors descend in silence, their shadows stretching long across the walls, flickering with the lit lanterns that guide their path. It opens at the bottom into a chamber carved directly from bedrock. The catacombs. Low arches hold the ceiling aloft. The walls are lined with shelves of smooth stone where the dead are laid to rest. Some marked, honoured with wooden plaques. Others with nothing at all.

Tilda follows behind them now, one hand on the walls for balance. She speaks only once. "There," her voice carries through the chamber, threatening to breathe life back into the bodies around them. She points to an empty niche near the back, "with the others."

The hunters lower the slab with careful hands. The wood settles against the stone shelf with a thud. Isaac lies, surrounded by the people who were sworn to protect him, sworn to show him how to fulfil his destiny.

Tilda steps forward and lays a cloth across his chest—the same golden sun spiral woven in the fabric catches the light from the lanterns, shimmering against it.

Alara watches the boy's face in the flickering light. The glow softens his features, illuminating his youth. His lashes curl against his cheeks. In the soft light, he appears to be sleeping. She stays behind as the others make their way back up to rejoin the village. Her chest tightens and the stillness presses down on her. No excuses. No rituals. Just the truth of what's been lost.

Her words barely form in the heavy silence of the catacombs. "I failed you." She brushes her hand across his delicate face. "I'm sorry."
She places one hand on the edge of the stone shelf. Her fingers curl around it, not wanting to let go but knowing they must.

She finally moves away and turns towards the steps, weathered by time and sorrow. She climbs them, putting out the lanterns on her way, leaving Isaac in the quiet dark. The dead remain asleep and the living carry their guilt back into the light.

By the time Alara has climbed the last of the stone steps, the clearing is empty. The wind has shifted, now cold and harsh. Auryn waits at the threshold, arms crossed, shoulders squared against the chill. "They've gone inside."

Inside the chapel, the scent of roasted meat hangs in the air. The space is warm and loud, the chatter forced and discordant. Laughter rings hollow. Mugs clink harshly against the tables, tradition clawing its way to the surface.

The feast is sparse. One whole pig, roasted over coals and carved thin. Bread stacked high on wooden platters. No cheese. No stew. The goats were lost to the NeedleTeeth. The fields too mangled for harvest. It's very clear the village is heading into a lean winter.

Plates are passed out in small, uneven portions, many of the villagers avoiding each other's eyes as they move along. Others murmur thanks like apologies.

There's warm ale, though. Plenty of that. Jugs line the long tables, their contents sloshing as they're poured and set down too roughly.

Alara grabs a plate from the edge of the table. The food is strewn about, barely enough to call it a meal. She follows Auryn to a seat at the far end of the hall.

Auryn pours her a mug without asking. She drinks it in one long pull. He pours another.

"How are you holding up?" he asks.

Alara pokes at the food on her plate.

"Probably as well as you are." Auryn nods slowly. He doesn't press any further. She's grateful for that.

In the far corner of the chapel by the hearth, Serilda sits alone. No plate. No mug. Her hands rest flat on her knees. She stares into the fire, her eyes fixated on it, not blinking.

Alara excuses herself and walks over to her. "Thank you for coming, Auntie," she says, lowering herself onto the bench beside her.

Serilda only nods. Her mouth twitches, shaping words on her tongue but they don't come.

Alara peers around the room, at the tribute of her people. Isaac's mother is absent. She hears quiet gossiping around the subject.

Alec sits on the other side of the room, squeezed between Deia and Emalie's family. He doesn't notice Alara watching him. He keeps his eyes on the small portion of bread and meat on his plate and shovels it into his mouth in greedy handfuls. Alara wants to go to him. She wants to sit at his side and run her fingers through his curls, to tell him everything he needs to hear. But she stays where she is. He hasn't spoken to her since the morning prior. Hasn't even glanced in her direction. So she watches from across the room. She watches those little hands dig into his food, stuffing his mouth like this is the last meal he'll ever eat.

Auryn moves towards her, weaving past villagers caught up in quiet conversation. He stops beside her, leaning over so no one else can hear him. "Want to get out of here?"

Alara nods and pushes herself from the bench she had been sharing with Serilda.

No one stops them. No one notices when they slip through the chapel doors, into the night. The feast carries on, like it always does. Because it must. Because the living remain.

The tavern is empty when they arrive. Even Benjamin and Risa are absent, still paying their respects at the feast. Auryn moves behind the bar without pause. He lifts a bottle from the display shelf, something dark and sharply scented and grabs two small glasses from beneath the counter. He returns to where Alara has settled into one of the stools, her elbows planted on the countertop.

He pours.

She drinks.

He pours another.

Alara finishes the second glass with ease. She sets it down, the burn still present in her throat. For a while, she just stares at the wood beneath her arms. It's scarred—each knife-carved groove a story—and waxy from years of ale and sweat. She wonders how many people have sat here, chasing some sort of peace, the way she does now.

She clears her throat. "Thank you."

Auryn glances over and raises an eyebrow. "For what?"

"I'm not sure exactly... just, thank you."

A smile spreads across his face. "I'm your friend, aren't I?" He bumps his shoulder into hers, playfully and pours her another drink.

"Yeah... you sort of snuck up on me."

"Sounds like me," he smirks, polishing off his glass. "I knew we'd be friends if you gave me the chance. Just like old times..."

She doesn't answer right away. She sits with it, turning her glass slowly in her hand. A long moment passes before she speaks again. "Do you ever feel like... I don't know... like there's something better out there?"

"Out where?"

She shrugs. "Anywhere. This village—it doesn't feel like home. Not really."

Auryn sets his glass down and turns to face her. No smile, no playful edge. His focus narrows as she speaks, listening with precision.

"It doesn't feel safe here," she continues. "It feels like everything around me keeps dying. Like we're cursed."

He nods slowly.

"We're down to the last of us. Hunters, I mean." Her voice falters. "There's only three of us left since Maren... Only one on the rise since Isaac... We're just supposed to wait to be picked off? One by one..."

Auryn lets out a soft, uneasy chuckle and slides the bottle an arm's length away. "Maybe we should put this down for now." He watches her for a moment before adding, "I get what you mean, though. My parents. Your mother... Isaac..." he swallows his grief at their names. "It all feels like one long nightmare."

"Do you miss them?"

"Everyday. A part of me wishes I could have been there. Maybe I could have—"

She cuts him off. "You were sixteen, Auryn. There's nothing you could have done. You weren't even done your training."

"I know. But what if..." he trails off, staring into nothing. He shakes his head and polishes off his drink. "Well, this wasn't the kind of evening I had in mind when I asked you to leave with me."

She breathes a quiet laugh. "What kind of evening *did* you have in mind?"

He looks at her, meeting her eyes with an unfamiliar softness. "You looked sad. I wanted to help."

Chapter Fourteen

Shadows dance between the windows against the warm amber of candlelight. A forced laughter echoes from the chapel, bouncing off the forest canopy before reaching Melinda's ears. She sits quietly on her doorstep, peering out to the feast, painfully aware of Isaac's absence.

Her mind wanders to terrible places. A dark gloomy wood, Isaac cornered, alone. She tightens her jaw and closes her eyes, allowing herself to drift to a happier place. A golden meadow, Isaac laughing and racing towards her. She smiles for a moment, before realizing she will never see his crooked grin again.

In the distance, a cry is formed, pulling Melinda from her daydream.

Isaac.

She perks up as the cry comes again and hops up to her feet, trailing towards it. It entrances her, leading her away from the warmth and laughter, away from the village. Under any other circumstance, Melinda knows better than to follow a mysterious call into the woods. But Isaac's familiar voice hypnotizes her, pulling at her grief.

She follows. Every ounce of logic has fled her mourning heart and truly a world without him in it is not enticing enough for her to regain it. On her sides, lights blur and vanish, the village slipping into the darkness behind her. Isaac cries out again, screaming her name and Melinda marches on.

The forest drowns her in shadow. It calls her in and she answers. Melinda's mind betrays her. She doesn't question his invitation as it chimes out from the cave. She steps inside.

As she enters, she sees him. Isaac. His back is turned to her, his short hair curling gently into the back of his neck. He wears a mud-stained tunic, tucked loosely into a ripped pair of linen trousers. She walks closer to him, kicking a loose stone across the ground and startling the boy. He jumps, turning swiftly. His face brightens and he stretches his arms out to greet her, an innocent smile plastered across him. Melinda breaks into a jog and races across the cave to embrace him.

"Mother!" he yells. "I knew you would come!" Melinda pulls him into a tight embrace, sobbing violently as she grabs at his face... neck... back.

"I'm here, baby," she cries between sobs. He beams at her for a moment and then steps back clumsily.

"I knew," he says, his cheekbones arching high and eyes slanting inwards, "that you," his hair grows long, twisting into brilliant curls and his stature shrinks, "would come." *Emalie* stares at Melinda, unblinking. Her chest stands firm. No breath emerges from her lungs. She wears an exaggerated smile, stretching beyond her normal span of lips. "Mother," she sings, her voice still masked as Isaac's, her arms still outstretched.

"Isaac?" she questions, backing away slowly.

"She said we'd be safe if we didn't leave," Emalie laughs. Melinda rubs her eyes and glances around the dark cave. "Don't you recognize me?" Emalie cackles as she morphs back into Isaac's form.

Melinda stares at the child, frozen, unable to respond. "It's dark here, Mommy," he cries. She flinches closer for a moment, then pulls back abruptly. He frowns. "Don't you love me anymore?" Melinda stares, bewildered. "Why did you let me die?" Melinda reaches out and pulls him to her.

She sobs into him, inhaling his scent. "I'm so sorry," she cries.

"You're not!" Isaac shouts. "Not yet." His voice echoes through the cave as he collapses into himself. Melinda holds her arms in place, an empty circle where his body stood just moments before.

"Baby!" she screams. He doesn't answer. She throws herself to the floor and begs him to return. A breeze howls through the cave, tousling her hair over her face. She twists around, clawing herself free. Laughter explodes, crackling through the air. "Please, come back to me!" she cries.

Silence falls around her.

The cave is painfully dark. Melinda darts her eyes around but she is unable to make anything out.

Across from her, a light flashes. It tears from one side of the cave to the other. Melinda sinks back and it flashes again, this time just above her. She looks upwards and the room fills with an ominous glow. Her eyes lock on shimmering black beads, staring back at her. The Fae crouches into the ceiling, enormous flesh-coloured wings stretching out at its sides. Its skin clings firmly to them, wrapped taut around thick ivory bones, spreading through the wings like veins. It peers down at her, swivelling its head in a full circle before singing, "Don't you love me anymore?" It digs its hind claws into the roof of the cave, flinging its body down and hanging before her like a bat. Melinda is unable to tear her eyes from its gaze. Its head spins around again, ending its rotation with Isaac's face. "Stay with me, Mommy," it begs in a borrowed voice. The Fae drops from the roof, wings outspread and hovers motionless before her. Isaac's face again disappears and it whispers menacingly, "Pain is for the living."

Melinda slams her eyes shut and clutches the spiralled sun pendant around her neck. She mutters to herself, causing the Fae to screech out. It slaps her hand down and tosses her against the wall.

"We don't like this game," Isaac and Emalie chime in unison. Melinda pulls herself back to her feet, the Fae scurrying into the darkness just beyond her.

"Isaac, I..."

"You can make it stop," the voice hisses. "Make *all* the pain disappear." The Fae pumps its wings, only twice, closing the gap between them. Melinda stares at the enormity of the creature. Its chest lifts in long, heavy swells, each breath stretched thin by the vastness of its lungs. The skin along the top of its head is cracked and dry, thorny brambles piercing through the flesh, growing upwards from within the Fae's skull to sprout an undeserved crown. It stares down at her with a venomous grin and whispers again, "Pain is for the living."

Melinda's mind jumps through muddled thoughts of Isaac and life at Ravenforge. She thinks about the pain his absence brings and finds herself considering the Fae's offer. She cannot endure this life without him by her side.

In the corner stands a dwarfed cliff, the tip of it no more than 10 feet from the ground.

Melinda notices it and the creature laughs at her contemplation. A thick threaded rope drops from the roof of the cave and dangles over the edge of the cliff, held in place by old magic and trickery. Melinda squints at it and Isaac runs over and takes her by the hand.

"I've been waiting so long, Mommy," he says. "Please don't leave me alone in the dark."

Melinda rips the sun charm from her throat and tosses it idly to the side. She walks slowly, each step coated with a mix of regret and eagerness. As she reaches the rope, she pulls it into her hands. She runs them along the fibres, each stroke pulling her closer to the edge.

"We can help you find the peace," sing Isaac and Emalie. "Stay with us."

Melinda looks down at her son beside her and smiles. Whatever this is, it's better than a life without him. She nods and moves to place the rope around her neck.

A shrill laughter explodes around her. It bounces off the walls, echoing through the shadows. It comes from every direction, closing in around her, mocking her. Melinda freezes and stares out into the dark. Two bony hands grab at her temples, their long fingernails curling around the base of her chin. Sharp claws dig into her, blood pooling around their tips. Melinda gasps and the Fae shrieks again. In one swift movement, it jerks its hands to the side, snapping her neck.

Melinda's body topples to the floor. Her head twists unnaturally to the side, severed bone piercing through the skin.

"That's better, *Mommy*," the Fae cackles, slinking back into the shadows, its nails clicking along the stone walls. "Did you really think you had a choice?"

Chapter Fifteen

Auryn and I are walking behind the old chapel. The sun is high and dull behind a thin veil of clouds. Neither of us speak. It's not uncomfortable, just quiet.

He walks a step ahead of me, hands in his pockets, head turned towards the trees. I don't know where we are going, though it doesn't seem to matter.

We pass a crooked tree that I don't remember.

Odd.

I've had the entirety of Ravenforge mapped since I was a little girl. Its branches are gnarled and leafless, clawing towards the sky like mangled arms. I stare at it, questioningly, then glance back to Auryn.

He's gone. I stop walking. The wind picks up, hot and strange against the back of my neck. I turn in a slow circle, trying to spot Auryn. But there's no sign of him. No footprints in the dirt where he had just been walking with me. Just the chapel, the tree, and the sky... The sky has gone orange. Not the warm orange of a sunset. The light stretches across the clouds, too bright. Too thick. Like molten glass over the sun. The clouds begin to swirl into themselves, rolling in slow spirals. The sky glows with them, a blaze that stains the earth below it.

The chapel appears scorched beneath the light. Darker. Older. Abandoned.

A sharp sound cuts through the stillness. Muffled but frantic—the slamming of fists against wood.

Thump. Thump. Thump.

It echoes in the pit of my stomach.

I hear a voice. Guttural and wet, as though it's been dragged through water and has still found the strength to scream.

"Alara!"

Alec.

His voice cracks on the words, high and panicked. "Help me!"

My feet carry me forward before I even think to move. The sky still burns above me, casting long, trembling shadows against the chapel walls.

"Alec?" I shout.

I stumble down the slope towards the back door. The banging continues, louder this time.

"Please! Alara! They're coming for me!" His voice is raw. Terrified. So close I can feel the vibrations around me.

I slam my shoulder into the door. It bursts open with a groan of the old hinges. Cold air floods over me, damp and stale. I take the stairs down, two at a time. The sound grows louder. Desperate. I reach the bottom and a misplaced door slams shut in front of me, so fast and hard the walls shake.

"Alec!" I scream, pounding on the wood. "I'm here!"

Alec is still screaming. He's trapped in the catacombs. I grab at the handle. I pull, twist, and shove my full weight into it. The door doesn't budge. I hurl myself at it. The wood turns to stone. I reach for the handle and it vanishes through my fingers. My breath catches and I fall to my knees as Alec continues to call for me.

"No..." I whisper. "Open, damn it, open!" Something inside me unravels. The words I whisper are foreign to me. They rise from my throat without shape, pouring out like blood. Urgent. Wild. Something old hums beneath each syllable. I place my hands on the door. The stone pulses beneath them.

Alec goes quiet.

The door begins to shiver. "Open!" I command it.

The door creaks open slowly before tumbling away altogether. The stone crumbles into the darkness like ruins. I stumble back as shadows begin to unfurl from within. They pour out across the floor like water. They wind around my ankles, through my hair, tousling it before slipping away. Something steps forward. A man. He's tall and dressed in dark robes that brush the ground. His hair is black, streaked grey at the temples. His features are sharp, elegant, and familiar.

I don't know him. But something inside of me does.

A slow smile curls his lips. "I knew you would do it," he says softly. He reaches out to me. Fingers, cold and steady, slide over the top of my head. The touch is soft, almost soothing.

A sound rises from behind him. Chittering. It floods the corridor in a violent surge—bones rattling, claws scraping, teeth gnashing. The walls crack open with the weight of them. The sound is everywhere—above, below, beside me.

NeedleTeeth pour out from all sides of the man. Dozens at first. Then more. Crawling over each other in a rush of limbs and teeth. They keep coming, clawing their way to freedom all around the man, leaving him untouched. He watches me with pride.

The creatures skitter across the floor, the walls, the ceiling. Their bodies slam into the archway as they claw themselves up towards the opening.

The chittering is unbearable. It isn't a sound anymore, it's a sensation. It fills my throat, my jaw, my chest. Like I've swallowed it. Like I'll never get it out.

The man steps forward, the corners of his mouth twitching with approval.

Cracks snake through the floor behind him, splitting with a pulsing fire. Light spills upwards from the stone, veins pumping, orange, red, and devouring. It matches the sky. Bleeding. Burning.

The man looks at me one last time, *smiling*.

A pounding at the door pulls Alara from her sleep. The nightmare still feels heavy in her chest. Her breathing comes in short bursts. She tries to calm herself.

Just a dream.

Feathers float around her. Another pillow down.

The rapping at the door grows louder. "Alara?" Deia's voice is rough and panicked. Alara shoots up from her bed and runs to the door, yanking it open. Deia stumbles back at the abruptness.

"What's wrong?" She sees the sky first. Orange. She steps outside, taking it in. Just like her nightmare, the clouds roll into themselves like dark red smoke, smothering the sun. "What—"

"She's gone," Deia says.

"Who's gone?"

"Melinda. I went to bring her something to eat and her door was open. She's not in the village. I've looked everywhere."

Alara stares at the sky and watches her people do the same. It's the colour of flame—deep molten orange laced with black and red. People gather in small, quiet clusters. Some look up with narrowed eyes, others scratch at their arms, their scalps, trying to make sense of the sight.

Alara blinks, shaking off the remnants of sleep. "Melinda—"

"She's *gone,*" Deia repeats, firmer now. Alara stands there, watching the sky. She rubs at her eyes trying to wake herself.

This can't be real.

"Alara! Melinda—"

"Belongs to the trees now, dear," Serilda cuts in gently, her voice light and distant.

The crowds around them stiffen. One by one, the people of Ravenforge begin to step away, uneasy glances passing between them. Most head back to their homes, closing their doors and drawing their curtains.

Deia moves uncomfortably, shifting her weight under both feet.

"She walks because they ask her to. She follows because they lie."

Alara looks to Deia, Serilda's mutterings barely phasing her. "Where is Alec?"

"Still sleeping," Deia answers, clearing her throat as her voice catches.

"Keep him inside until we know what's happening."

Deia doesn't argue. "Gladly. I'll... I'll stay with him." She turns and walks back to her cottage, thankful for the excuse to leave.

Alara steps out further, still watching the sky. Serilda follows at her side.

"He came to you last night. Did you let him out?"

Alara's brows furrow. "What? Who—"

"What's going on?" Auryn jogs up from behind, his eyes locked on the sky. Bram follows closely. Both of them stare upwards, their expressions darkening.

The clouds above them continue to roll and twist like flames, thick and alive.

"What is this?" Bram mutters.

"I don't know," Alara says.

"Oh, you do," Serilda's voice chimes in. "You only refuse to see it."

Alara turns to her. "What? I don't—"

Something moves at the tree line. A shadow. Thin, darting, gone again with her next breath.

Alara's heart lurches. She spins and bolts back to her cottage, grabbing the dagger from her bedside. She doesn't stop to breathe. She's already running.

"Alara!" Auryn calls, startled.

"Wait!" Bram shouts after her.

She's already gone.

Branches snap under her boots and thorns dig into her arms as she pushes through the underbrush. She catches another glimpse of the figure. A shadow, narrow and uneven, weaving through the trunks.

Bare feet? A pale leg?

It moves fast but doesn't seem to be running. It drifts forward, just out of reach. Alara's lungs burn with cold air but she doesn't stop. The trees grow closer, tighter. Light flickers in narrow beams from the canopy above, painted in orange and crimson from the sky. The figure flickers ahead again. Alara's foot catches a root. She stumbles, catching herself on a nearby trunk and continues the chase.

"Melinda?" she calls, breathless. "Stop!"

The figure doesn't answer, moving deeper still. It curves around a bend and disappears again. Alara presses on, panting, ducking beneath low branches.

"Melinda!" She calls louder.

She pushes through a thicket of thorns and stumbles into a hollow where the trees split just enough to let the bleeding sky spill through.

Something sits at the base of a tree. Alara skids to a stop.

Lily.

Her small body leans against the bark, her legs stretching before her on the ground. Her head is tilted upwards, face calm. She's staring at the sky with milky eyes. Above them the clouds ripple and twist—thick as smoke, slow as oil.

Alara studies her face. The way her sightless eyes seek to track the sky's chaos above. How it entrances her. She blinks, unable to process what's happening. A strange chill crawls down her spine. Before she can step closer, something moves between the trees ahead. Alara tears her eyes away from Lily and follows.

She calls out again, "Melinda!" She ducks a low branch and stops there.

The figure is still in front of her. It turns its head, long enough to get a good look. What turns to face her is not Isaac's mother. A tangle of dark hair clings to its back and shoulders. The woman's face is bare and weathered with hollow sockets where the eyes should be. Her jaw hangs crooked, parted slightly. Alara doesn't breathe as the figure turns again and keeps moving.

"Mama...?"

Am I dreaming?

The thought lands like a stone in her chest.

The sky.

Lily.

Mama.

None of it makes any sense.

Behind her she can hear Bram and Auryn's voices, distant and muffled.

She doesn't wait for them. She can't. Her mind is set, her dagger ready in her hand. She claws her way up a hill, following her mother over it. Alara stumbles into a clearing—and stops. She knows this place. The earth is still bruised where the blood has soaked in. This is where they found them. Emalie curled up against that same stone slab. Maren crouched over Isaac's body.

She scans the area, her eyes catching the silhouette vanishing behind a tangle of black roots. She moves carefully towards it, inspecting the space. What had appeared to be a mess of roots and vines is more than that. An opening. A cave mouth, narrow and low. Dark.

Alara grips her dagger tightly and steps inside. She squints against the blackness, trying to make sense of the shape that stands before her. It's slim and wrapped in shadows. She takes another cautious step forward. Behind her, Bram and Auryn push through the curtain of vines and roots, allowing orange light to spill in, long enough to get a glimpse.

Melinda.

Her head is cocked to the side at a grotesque angle. Her lips are drawn back in a menacing grin too wide for her face. A shard of bone pokes out from the space her neck should be.

"What the fuck?" Bram breathes, taking in the sight before him.

Melinda continues to grin at them—head crooked, bone jutting from her throat. She giggles. It's gentle at first, soft enough to be mistaken for a breath.

It grows louder, sounding almost childlike but something in it warps on the way out. It bounces off the walls of the cave, trailing into a rasp that scrapes the stone. Without warning, Melinda drops to all fours and scuttles into the dark. The shadows swallow her whole in a single beat. Gone before the hunters have a chance to react.

Auryn steps towards Alara. His eyes are locked on the dark ahead, searching for movement of any kind.

A second giggle slips around them. This one more feral than the last. There's a scraping along the roof, the walls, beneath them. The creature moves fast. Too fast. Too many limbs. Nails or bones click against stone, dragging over it. The sound rushes across the walls, zipping from one end of the cave to the other—above them, behind them, below them. Just out of reach.

A spark catches Alara's eye to the left. She sees a glimpse of a nail, too long to belong to anything human. "It's playing with us."

Another giggle breaks through. This one comes with a voice, several voices, all speaking together as one. Melinda's voice twisted and singsong. A child's whisper. A man's low snarl. And one that makes Alara's blood run cold. Her mother's. "Don't you want to play?"

Alara's eyes start to adjust to the dark. A shape clings to a far corner of the cave's ceiling. Its thin limbs are hooked into the stone. Its body is

long, curled into itself like a resting spider. Alara squints hard, her breath straining when she sees it.
Wings.
Flesh-coloured and large, twitching with a feral anticipation.
Her throat closes around the word. "Fae."
Auryn shifts closer to Alara, placing himself between her and the Fae. It laughs at the sentiment. A low, warped sound, stretched from too many mouths at once.
The creature twists backwards and skitters down a far passage, inviting them in.
Alara moves to follow. Auryn catches her arm swiftly. "No." His voice is steeped in sharp panic.
"That *thing* has my mother's voice. Do you know what that means?" She shakes him off and throws herself down the tunnel.
Auryn rolls his head back and lets out a growl through his teeth, the kind of sound only frustration and fear in tandem can make. "Damn it, Alara!" He sprints into the dark after her.
"We don't know how to kill it!" Bram calls after them.

The tunnel stretches ahead, short and narrow, twisting into paths carved by something that has never walked upright. Auryn moves fast, forced to duck as he runs, trying to keep up with Alara in the dark. The tunnel yawns into a small chamber, ribbed with stone and low hanging roots.

Three paths split off before him—jagged mouths of shadow to the left, right, and straight ahead from where he stands.

He halts, his chest rising in sharp bursts. The silence is thick, the darkness even thicker. He turns his head... left... right... All three tunnels mirror the other.

"Alara?" he whispers quietly, his voice echoing with uncertainty. He turns in place, eyes scanning the tunnels, indecision tightening in his spine.

Movement flickers down the rightmost passage. It vanishes around a bend, too fast to distinguish. He hesitates for a brief moment before following, pulling his axe from his back as he moves.

The tunnel narrows further, damp walls pressing in. What began as a stride becomes a shuffle. The ceiling dips lower, forcing his head down. The walls creep inwards and before long he's turning his body sideways to squeeze through, scraping his shoulders on rough stone in the process. He grits his teeth as he continues.

He can hear movement somewhere ahead. The soft sound of something dragging, the faint clatter of stone being disturbed. He calls out to Alara again. A giggle curls through the quiet in response.

The walls press in further against him, on both sides now. His hands search them for any kind of break or turn, praying for some sort of release ahead. He forces himself to continue into the cramped space before the walls start to peel back. Subtly at first. He lets out a sigh of relief as the ceiling begins to lift and his steps are able to stretch out. The chamber breathes wider with each step he takes.

Light spills in up ahead, vivid and seething orange. The light flickers across the stone, like flames licking the earth, painting everything in hues of blood and ember.

Auryn stops at a small mouth at the end of the tunnel, squinting against the heatless glow. Something moves outside of the opening. His legs carry him forward, hoping to find Alara, safe and waiting for him.

Alara keeps her eyes fixed on the pale shape writhing ahead, its movements almost hypnotic. It glides effortlessly across the ceiling, twisting and folding into itself with unnatural grace.

Her boots slam the ground, her heart thundering behind her ribs, as she continues to chase down the creature that has stolen her mother's voice.

It speaks, taunting her. "Alara..." The voice is soft and familiar. "Come find me, darling."

Her breath catches with fury. "Let her go!"

The Fae lets out a rasping giggle that echoes around her, bouncing off the tunnel walls, coming at her from every direction at once.

She pushes harder, deeper into the dark, watching the Fae's pale skin flicker along the walls and ceiling. It veers left around a bend and she follows. Her foot catches on something soft blocking her way. She lurches forward on her hand and knees, pain exploding on the impact.

Alara hisses and rolls to her side, flicking her eyes downwards...

It lies on the floor before her.

Melinda.

Her body has been dumped in the narrow hall, twisted and broken. She appears nearly decapitated. A jagged bone juts from the side of her neck, punching through the skin. Alara stares, frozen. The imitation wasn't a disguise to throw them off.

It was a trophy.

Alara's fingers tighten around the hilt of her dagger as she rises, steadying her breath. She wipes the sting from her eyes with the back of her sleeve and wills herself forward. She doesn't have time to mourn. The creature wearing her mother's voice is still down here. And she intends to silence it.

She pushes on, turning into a narrow offshoot tunnel. The walls lean in closer the further she moves, before opening into a damp low niche.

The Fae waits for her, wrapped in darkness.

Alara's dagger begins to glow as she panics, illuminating the space. She lifts it, using the green light to inspect the shape before her. She nearly drops the blade at the sight of it. It's wearing her mother's skin. She appears whole. Alive. Her dark hair is braided back, just how she used to wear it on her hunts. Her mouth curls in a soft smile, sadness haunting the edges.

"It's alright, darling," the creature says, wearing Lyssa's voice like a mask. "Mama's here now."

Alara's stomach knots. "You are *not* my mother!" She points the blade at it, ready to strike.

Lyssa giggles softly. She takes a step forward and sniffs at the air. "Your soul... it smells... different."

Alara recoils.

The Fae notices. "You didn't know?" it laughs in Lyssa's voice. "She never told you," it says in a singsong manner.

Alara steadies herself, holding her blade tight. "Let her go," she commands.

Her mother's brow furrows. "But she tastes so good."

"I'm going to kill you!" Alara screams.

Lyssa blinks—slowly, deliberately. Her eyelids rise to reveal gaping sockets—twin wells of blackness. Her skin loses its colour just as quick, sagging and bloated like wet parchment paper. The soft smile she wore seconds ago collapses. Her lips peel back as her jaw drops into a silent gaping scream. The Fae lets out a delighted laugh. "You don't want to stay with us?" Its taunt is fractured, her mother's voice lying beneath something else, something wrong. A whisper beneath a shriek. Its skin seems to slough off entirely, folding in on itself like a curtain drawn too fast.

The creature that remains is something pulled from the deepest, cruellest parts of the woods. Long limbs with joints that bend the wrong way. Its skin is like bleached bark, with large black eyes that shimmer in the dagger's light. It hovers, weightless in front of her.

Alara swings her dagger out and catches its arm. The steel kisses its flesh. The Fae lets out a warbling scream, dozens of voices melding together as one. Steam hisses violently from the wound. It reels back. Its clawed hand curls over the burn. Its expression cracks long enough for Alara to see.

Fear.

Bram stands alone at the mouth of the cave. The others have gone, swallowed by darkness and amateur impulse. He should go after them. He should do something. But he cannot afford that. He stays there, telling himself to wait.

Just a little longer.

The quiet feels too heavy now, like the silent pause before the thunder.

Alara had charged in without thinking, as she always does. And Auryn followed behind seconds later with just as much thought to it.

He shifts his weight uncomfortably, glancing once towards the path Alara and Auryn disappeared down. He holds his blade in his hand, his palm damp with sweat. He lingers at the tunnel's entrance. One step forward means chasing death. One step back means abandoning them. He continues to watch the empty corridor, struggling against himself. Finally, he shakes his head and curses under his breath. He's made his mind up. He's leaving. Ravenforge cannot suffer the loss of all three of them. He turns to go. His foot barely touches the ground when a soft voice follows from behind.

"Bram...? My dear boy?" The words drift through the dark. Soft and delicate. And unmistakenly hers.

He stops in his tracks and turns, slowly, to the sound, his pulse kicking in his throat. "Mum?"

Standing just beyond the frame of the tunnel is his mother. A knitted shawl hangs loose around her shoulders, her dark hair tied low in a messy knot. Her brows are drawn in confusion. She blinks at him, dazed. "How... How did I get here?"

Bram's heart skips at the sight of her. He stays there, frozen, refusing to accept what stands before him as truth.

His mother hacks into her sleeve, blood staining the fabric. "Help me," she pleads as she stumbles to the floor. Bram jumps towards her, his instinct to tend to her sickness stronger than his urge to flee. He holds her gingerly, fearful of her delicate condition. She coughs into his shoulder, grasping his shirt as she chokes on her own saliva.

"We need to get you out of here," he says, brushing the loose strands of hair from her sweat-slicked cheeks. "You need your medicine."

"I need... you to stay... Stay with me..."

Bram stiffens at her words. He does not move. He does not dare breathe. He stares down at her, waiting for whatever comes next.

She begins to laugh, a layered manic laugh. Too many voices mixed together to create a sickening sound. A deep incision starts from the corner of her mouth, something unseen splitting the skin all the way to her ear. The flesh hangs there, curling outwards, exposing muscle and bone. Bram stares in shock as the laughter continues. Between the cracks of her laughter, blood begins pouring from her mouth. Her shawl rips violently from her shoulders, the thread shredded down the center. Bram steps backwards, his eyes fixed on his mother. She stretches her left arm downwards, the skin growing thin. Veins and muscle throb beneath it. She laughs as her arm pops, snapping free from her shoulder and flies across the space.

"Stop it!" he shouts, his eyes slick with tears. The laughter bellows, rippling over the stone surrounding them. The Fae rises to its feet before him, gliding upright, towering over him as he remains still. The illusion of his mother peels away. What's left behind is sickly and distorted. It grows taller, its limbs lengthening in seconds. It smiles at him with a grin so wide and out of place it leaves a sinking feeling in the pit of his stomach.

Bram doesn't run. His legs won't answer. He braces, watching the thing draw back its claws, ready to strike.

A high piercing shriek slices through the dark. The Fae jolts. Its head snaps towards the sound, nostrils flaring, neck twisting in a primal animalistic jerk. A second shriek follows, louder than the first. It lingers, vibrating off the damp cavern walls. Bram feels it rattle deep in his chest. The Fae standing before him starts screaming in unison, so violently it contorts its whole body.

Something barrels out of the tunnel—slim, pale, and screeching. Bram throws his hands over his ears, slamming the weight of them into his skull. Alara pursues it, her eyes locked, wild with fury.

Three more Fae burst from the shadows behind her. The air ignites with movement as they take to the ceiling, wings unfurling in a blur of motion. They circle in a frenzy, howling and clawing at the stone above. Dust and debris rain down on the two hunters as they spiral overhead. Bram ducks instinctively, pressing his back to the wall as The Swarm tightens.

Alara catches his eye amidst the chaos. "Where's Auryn?"

"He isn't with you?" Bram shouts.

A clawed foot drops from the ceiling, hooking around Alara's arm, jerking her upwards. She snarls at it and drags her dagger across the creature's ankle. The blade sears through its flesh. The Fae screams and releases her. A chorus of shrill, ear-splitting wails fill the chamber, the kind that rattles teeth and burrows into bone.

Alara slashes at the space above her in hopes of inflicting more damage on The Swarm. Bram barrels into her, grabbing her around the waist and yanking her towards the exit.

"Not now!" he barks, dragging her through the narrow mouth of the cave and into the blinding orange haze outside.

The sky blazes above them. Alara whirls and drops to one knee, reaching into the small satchel around her waist. She scatters iron shavings in a thick, jagged line across the entrance, trapping The Swarm inside.

The screeching stops. Silence falls in its place.

Five pairs of eyes ignite from the darkness—black obsidian, like stars dipped in ink. The sky's amber glow radiates off them, pulsing slightly as the Fae track their retreat down the tunnel before disappearing altogether.

A twig snaps to the right. Alara turns sharply, her blade ready in her hand.

Auryn emerges from the far edge of the cave. His eyes catch on Alara and Bram and for a split second something resembling joy breaks through the exhaustion. "Oh, thank Gods," he shouts. His eyes glance between the cave and the pouch Alara clutches on her waist. The air carries the subtle, metallic scent of iron. He laughs awkwardly, a relieved smile blooming on his lips.

"Auryn!" A shaky breath escapes Alara.

"Quick thinking with the iron," Auryn muses.

Bram inhales sharply through his nose. "It doesn't smell like rain. They won't be able to cross for now."

"It'll give us a head start back to Ravenforge, at least," Alara adds.

"That was too close!" Auryn chuckles, continuing to close the distance between them. "There's going to be a whole council meeting about th—"

Something cuts across the orange-lit stone.

Lily.

She hurls her body at Auryn, jaw unhinged, snapping towards his throat. The jagged remnants of her teeth sink into his flesh. Auryn has no chance to react, no reflex to predict Lily's unprovoked violence.

A sickening crunch fills the gap between the hunters. Auryn jerks violently as Lily tears away his throat, leaving behind nothing but the glossy white of his spine. Blood spurts out from the wound. Auryn's eyes open impossibly wide and he falls to the ground. His limbs twitch unrhythmically at his sides before falling still. Lily jumps on top of him, biting into his face, furiously gnawing at the exposed skin.

A hush captivates the forest, silencing the birds and the breeze. Time slows and the woods blur around them, as if the trees are holding their breath.

The silence breaks.
Alara screams.

PART TWO

CHAPTER I

"Stop pushing!" The sting of the words hung in the air as instinct overwhelmed and took control. Ysabel rushed to Aveline's side, dabbing the sweat from her forehead with a crusty towel, while screams erupted around her. Aveline lay helpless on the bed, her bare knees high in the air.

This should be a joyous day, their first look upon the heir she had been brewing the past nine months. Rather, there was a sense of dread in the room. Aveline hadn't felt the baby move for days. Hadn't felt a single flutter in her swollen belly, leaving the happiness of their first meeting tainted with the unspoken knowledge that this child was not promised. That his life may be nothing but a blink.

Again, the screams filled the room, only now Aveline realized they were coming from her.

"You must not push!"

Those words again.

Aveline's body would not obey, tensing with each contraction, desperate to evict the child from its womb.

Aveline muttered to herself, a prayer she had learned as a young girl, one that was promised to lead her and her unborn child through this torment unscathed. She glanced around the room, her eyes settling upon the doctor's face.

His mouth curled in anguish and he gestured towards Ysabel. Ysabel dropped the towel in her hand and rushed to his side. He whispered to her. Aveline locked her eyes on them, straining to hear the words being spoken, her body betraying her with another contraction. She screamed as the room began to spin around her. Stuck battling with her body, urging it to keep her son safe.

"Footling presentation—" she heard as her eyelids drooped and then quickly flickered back open, "—be a miracle."

Had she been granted a moment to feel it, Aveline would have cried for the sake of the child but relentlessly, her body tightened. Pain surged through her, an unimaginable pain, forcing her to grit her teeth and pull at her hair. Still, it was nothing compared to the pain of her lost babies that came before.

Aveline's gaze shifted to Ysabel and just then the gratitude she felt for her sister was overwhelming. Aveline admired her angelic appearance—her golden blonde locks and gentle green eyes. She stood barefoot in her flowing white nightdress, never expressing complaint through the long hours of her labour. Aveline felt a smile touch her lips for a brief moment, before the pain set in again and those cracked lips parted to release a visceral scream. Blood sprayed out from between her legs, splattering Ysabel's white dress with crimson red streaks. The doctor's eyes widened and he backed away from the table. He shook his head in a sombre silence and quickly fled the room.

    Aveline felt the muscles in her stomach loosen as the tension in her body disappeared. Ysabel stood stiff by her side, her lips puckered and breath frozen in her chest. The air was silent. Aveline glanced down and saw her child's body sprawled at the end of the bed. Not a son at all but a daughter, more beautiful than any she had ever seen. Mustering up the little strength she had left, Aveline perked herself up on her elbows, straining to gain a better look upon her. Her eyes settled on little toes and tiny curled up fingers, filling her with a love so primitive and desperate.

    Aveline reached her arms out towards the child but Ysabel quickly placed herself between them. She wrapped her in a gentle silk, scooping her up and hurrying off in the same direction the doctor had swiftly retreated.

Aveline looked around the empty room, the silence piercing her mind. She glanced between the paintings of her ancestors, hung deliberately around the bedchamber. Warm candlelight flickered the walls around them, filling their faces with an undeserved calm.

It took a moment for her to notice the blood-soaked sheets she rested upon. Once she did, her legs began to tremble and her breath quickened. She opened her mouth and tried to call out, twisting her body and pulling herself over to the edge of the bed. Aveline swung her right leg to the side and wobbled down to the ground, while the other leg flopped useless on the bed behind her.

Aveline was exhausted and broken but she craved her daughter's touch and it flooded her with a determination so strong, nothing could stop her. She willed her left leg into cooperation as it slid slowly across the bed, reluctantly joining its twin on the cold stone. Triumphantly, Aveline pulled herself to her feet.

She took a clumsy step forward and then another. The door was mere inches away. She could do this. She had to do this.

Aveline took another step as the room began to fade around her. She felt the warm gush of blood spill down her legs and the darkness closing in. She leaned forward, hand outstretched, sure that if she could only escape her bedchamber, everything would be alright.

 Aveline knew this to be true. Even as she felt her back slam into the hard stone beneath her, as she felt the familiar trickle of blood flow delicately down her forehead, she knew that everything would be fine. It had to be fine.

 Aveline's torso scraped along the damp ground, her skin pierced with dagger-like splinters of wood, as she was dragged backwards. She heard the familiar creek of their home's oak door behind her as it drew her body into its call. Aveline did not want to answer, yet she continued to travel towards it, its sound growing louder, until she felt the blunt weight of it slam into her hip. The brisk Autumn air slapped her cheeks and her nose filled with the sweet smell of freshly cut hay. Her eyelids twitched slightly as she tried to call out, the subtle clue that she had survived the night.

 It went unheard.

 A scream brewed in Aveline's chest but its desperation was not enough to surface it.

 She was alone. Not in body but in spirit.

 She wondered what fate awaited her, her faint pulse throbbing only for her young daughter. She longed to hold her just once, to breathe in her smell and run her fingers through the thick, black hair she had caught only a glimpse of hours before. Aveline's lips parted slightly as she tried to shout to her. Again, no noise came, only this time she heard a reply.

A rugged voice crackled through the breeze, shrouded by the deep breath of exhaustion and grief. "Toss her over there," it commanded. Aveline felt the pinching grip tighten beneath her arms as her body crashed into the brittle crunch of straw and mud.

"Do you want to say any words?"

"No. Leave the wretched witch. Luck be we don't torch her." The voices faded into the howling wind, leaving Aveline truly alone in the damp cold.

Time dissolved into blackness, Aveline surfacing in brief, hazy fragments, her mind a drifting blur of awake and unconsciousness. As she floated there, she felt a serene sense of peace enshrouding her, the troubles of her world a forgotten memory.

Once the cold returned and the darkness had loosened its grip, her eyes flickered open, revealing a blur of colours and shapes, as if she had opened them beneath deep water. Her chest felt the weight of it around her. She wiggled her fingers slightly. Strength was not a privilege she could currently afford but the awakening sent shivers through her body and she needed to feel anything else. Aveline rolled her head gently, her hair rubbing against the bed of straw beneath her. Her body ached but it was alive.

Somehow.

Her lips cracked and flaked, her tongue swollen, sticky and dry in her mouth. She glanced around the room, her eyes settling on a nearby trough. Aveline pulled her body towards it and threw her head beneath the water. The chill sent a sensation across her skin.

I am alive.

She drank slight sips, lingering her face beneath the water's surface, before returning upwards as her lungs began to beg for new air. Rubbing her eyes, Aveline spun herself around and glanced truly upon her surroundings.

Golden light filtered in through the slots of the dampened fence she had helped her husband build years ago. The ground lay churned, spotted with clumps of hay and fresh hoofprints around her. She heard a familiar snort and turned to see her beloved Bayard by her side, his lips vibrating with the sound. Aveline felt comforted by his presence. She recalled their last ride together, only a fortnight ago.

She had escaped to him from her bedchamber as the moon shone down, illuminating the crop fields surrounding them. Aveline had promised her husband she would not venture outside of the property with their heir so close to drawing his first breath. But she was unable to overcome the craving and off Aveline and Bayard had ridden into the night.

Aveline could smell the heavenly berries before she could see them and her body sighed with relief as they approached. She tore from the saddle with less care than one would expect given her state, yet she was graceful as she leapt. She plucked a berry from the bush and eagerly tossed it into her mouth. The sweet taste offered a brief respite from the aching pains that came with the task of creating new life. Aveline offered a handful of berries to Bayard as well but he refused them. She knew he would.

Aveline smiled at the memory and felt her stomach grumble. Bayard whinnied, a sort of sadness behind it but Aveline continued to smile. She felt oddly at peace, even as the realization hit her that she had been abandoned in this place.

The smell of horse manure wafted through the air, the stench of it causing her stomach to pang. She did not try to rid herself of it. Rather, she lay peacefully on the damp floor and rubbed her stomach tenderly, unable to yet face her daughter's cruel fate.

The memory of it came to her in waves.

A doctor's furrowed brow.

A splattered crimson streak.

She winced as they appeared, begging her mind to end the suffering.

A soft silk.

A stolen child.

Aveline's smile had disappeared, in its place a gruelling scream, as she laid her eyes upon her sweet babe, tossed into a corner, like a forgotten trinket. The child's black hair twisted around its face and its arms lay stretched out unnaturally. Aveline struggled to her feet and ran to the child's side.

    She pulled her into her arms, squeezing her frozen body against her chest. Aveline wrapped her in her warmth, rubbing the babe's back vigorously but it was to no avail. The child lay still, the body absent a beating heart.

    Aveline sobbed as she rocked back and forth. She hummed a comforting lullaby. One her mother had sung to her and her mother before that. As she hummed, she pulled herself to her feet, cradling her daughter—*her Iris*—delicately in her arms and started towards home.

    The sun blared down on Aveline as she marched. Her lost strength had returned, anger coursing through her nearly hollow veins. After all they had endured, Aveline could hardly fathom this cruelty.

    Aveline's husband, Edric, had loved her tenderly throughout the miscarriages. He had shown her kindness and carried her through those trying times.

    He had held her, many months ago, as she whimpered when she missed her monthly sickness, paralyzed by the fear of losing yet another babe.

Aveline had not imagined Edric capable of such betrayal. Their sweet daughter, born silent in the night... and tossed mindlessly aside.

And what of myself?

How could Edrick so plainly toss his doting wife to the elements, bleeding and dying, after they had just started their family?

The rage boiled in her chest, growing stronger with each deliberate step. Aveline's arms tightened around Iris, engulfing her in the steel blanket that was a mother's love. She shuddered as she thought about the time her daughter had spent helpless and alone while she lay there unconscious.

Someone has to pay.

The sun was setting from the sky when Aveline approached the oak door. It had taken her much longer to cross the fields than on any normal day and her arms ached under the weight of Iris. Her stomach throbbed, begging her to abandon this task and seek out food but she knew it was her duty, so she continued forward.

The oak door's creak announced her arrival. Edric and Ysabel sat side by side in the dining hall, a feast of mutton, bread and ale spread before them.

The pair looked up at the noise. Ysabel's attention darted to Aveline's face and she jumped to her feet, her eyes widened.

Aveline had been asleep for some time. Her dark hair was a tangled mess strewn with hay and sticks but her features were recognizable, nonetheless.

"Sister!" Ysabel gasped. "We thought... I... you were dead."

Aveline smiled sweetly at her younger sister. At least she knew she had not betrayed her.

Her smile vanished as Edric rose from the table. "You must not be here," he bellowed. Aveline winced at the sound, his voice pulling her back to the barn she had awoken in hours before. *Leave the wretched witch* he had ordered.

Aveline couldn't understand how her husband had been replaced with this cold and cruel man who now stood before her. Tears welled behind her eyes but Aveline forced them back down. She would not cry. Not in front of him. Not after what he had done. She demanded answers.

Tightening her stance and planting both feet firmly into the ground, Aveline opened her mouth to speak but she was only able to muster one word. "Why?"

Edrick scoffed at the sound of her frail voice. He slammed his fists down on the dark wooden table before him. The noise echoed throughout the room, causing both Aveline and Ysabel to jump in surprise. "Dammit woman!" he shouted, saliva spewing from his mouth, "I said *leave*!"

Ysabel opened her mouth in protest but quickly closed it again, fear silencing her words. Her eyes darted down to the floor as she stepped behind Edrick, his body serving as a shield between the sisters.

Aveline swallowed. Her throat was a giant lump of fright and betrayal. She wanted to run. But she was a mother now. And she had a duty. "We won't," her voice boomed.

This seemed to catch Edrick off guard. It was then that he noticed the bundle tucked up in Aveline's arms.

Edrick's face contorted as if possessed by a demon of revulsion. Horrified, he gazed upon his wife, cradling the body of their deceased child. His voice was vacant and unforgiving, "You get that Devil's brat off my homestead." Aveline didn't move. "Cursed she is. As are you, *witch!* Be gone!"

"Her name is Iris," Aveline snapped, turning for the door.

CHAPTER II

A storm was brewing overhead. Thick, black clouds painted the sky, soaking Aveline in freezing rain as the wind stirred through her wet, muddy hair. She moved swiftly to the closest neighbouring home, rapping on the door in a panic.

The door opened a sliver, just enough for her dear friend Tessa to get a good look at her. Her lips parted, her dark eyes masked with fear.

"Whom is it?" Tessa's husband barked through the warmth inside.

Tessa called back, her voice shaking as she spoke. "J-just Ysabel, dear. Asking for prayer for her unfortunate sister."

"Be hasty, woman!" he shouted as Tessa slid through the door, shutting it behind her. She shivered at the nip of the breeze against her exposed skin, the silk of her gown offering her no warmth. Aveline stepped to her side, ducking beneath the threshold, gifting herself a slight relief from the cold.

Tessa straightened, her eyes narrowing as she looked Aveline over. Her gaze fell to the babe clutched tightly to her chest. "You must go," she pleaded, her eyes now fixed to the ground. "Leave this place."

Aveline shook her head in disbelief. "We will die out there, Tessa," she cried, squeezing her arms tighter around Iris. "You cannot cast us away."

Aveline's closest friend crossed her arms and lowered her voice. "The both of you should have been dead already." Tessa's voice, usually kind and reassuring, was now frigid and threatening. She stepped back inside as her husband called for her again. She tightened her shoulders, peering nervously behind her.

"Please—" Aveline begged.

Tessa shook her head and turned back to face her. "Get that thing off my porch before I alert your husband."

Aveline opened her mouth in protest but Tessa slammed the door, leaving mother and daughter alone with nothing but the cold and the harsh echo of betrayal from those she had trusted most.

Lightning crashed above as Aveline trudged through the mud pits neighbouring her farm. She examined her surroundings, looking for shelter to wait out the storm. In the distance, a wolf howled. The sound made Aveline's skin shiver as she tightened her clutch on Iris. These woods were not safe—never safe.

Her stomach grumbled as she came to the edge of a creek. Aveline could not recall one so close by but she did not venture away from the property boundaries often. Dipping her hand below the surface, Aveline scooped the water to her lips, slurping it vigorously. The wolf's cry pierced the air yet again, shouting out towards the full moon perched high in the sky.

Hungry as she was, shelter was the top priority. Food would come but Iris needed protection from the elements.

The pair continued their walk through the thick forest, branches and undergrowth slowing their step. Aveline squinted her eyes as she looked out into the brush. Lightning flashed again, illuminating the sky just long enough for Aveline to catch a glimpse of a rough shelter on the horizon. That was it, the direction she needed to push her shaking legs forward. The night's sanctuary.

The shelter was loose and small. A fragile nest of sticks and shadows, held together by will and a ragged rope tied clumsily around the top. It was anything but elegant but it would keep them dry enough and was low to the ground—low enough to avoid the strikes of lightning around them. Aveline squeezed Iris tightly before lessening her grip and laying her across her lap.

She looked down upon her perfectly still face, tracing her features with her finger. She smiled and began to hum. The soft lullaby offered a soothing release as the familiar tune floated between Aveline and Iris. Aveline's eyelids became heavy and began to droop. Within moments, she was asleep.

Morning broke with the melody of a songbird, fresh dew clinging to the leaves around her. Aveline's stomach ached beneath her dampened clothing but the sun's sky offered a dull, comforting warmth. Dizzy and parched, she hoisted herself to her feet in search of food.

Rocking Iris delicately, she shuffled towards a thick patch of greenery adjacent the shelter. Fate smiled down upon her as she pushed aside branches to reveal a blackberry-freckled bush.

After Aveline had filled her belly, she glanced down upon Iris. The sweet taste of the berries still clung to her tongue and she felt her stomach flutter with the excitement of sharing it with her daughter.

Aveline pulled at the shoulder of her torn blouse. The air felt cool and sharp as it hit her skin. Her breasts were plump and sore, filled with milk and thick spiderwebbed veins. With all the babes lost, Aveline's body had never come far enough along to produce. She whispered a soft prayer, a thank you for this gift she had been given, before raising Iris to meet it.

Aveline had not been through this part of motherhood before but she did have faint memories of her own mother's struggles to feed Ysabel that she could lean on. Tilting Iris's head back slightly in her palm, she pressed her nipple, cracked and dry, between her frigid lips.

Aveline gasped at the sharp sting. Supporting Iris's head in her arm, she squeezed her breast with her right hand, kneading it with her fingers. They were tender to the touch but Aveline embraced the pain, pressing hard as she felt her milk drop. Her nipples tingled terribly as she felt the heavy pull above her collarbone but relief washed over her as the milk began to flow. Aveline watched Iris's cheeks, filling like little pouches, warm milk trickling past the crease of her purple lips.

She looked down on Iris and noticed how similar her features looked to those of her younger sister.

Aveline's mind wandered back to her childhood, to the memory of Ysabel and her mother cuddled together on Ysabel's first night. Her mother's skin sparkled, dampened with sweat, as she fought her youngest daughter to take a drink. Ysabel had struggled to latch, throwing her head angrily from side to side, desperate for a drink but too eager and inexperienced to find it.

Iris drank with much more ease. Aveline smiled to herself as she felt her breasts deflating. Iris didn't fuss, she didn't lash her head around but Aveline swore she felt the weight of her gentle suckle as she drank.

Iris's body was stiff and Aveline could not feel the pumping of her heart over the whooshing of her breasts releasing but she didn't mind. This baby was not perfect but she was hers and Aveline would love her—despite her flaws.

Day turned to night, night to day, as Aveline and Iris pressed on. It would have been easy for her to surrender to the forest, to allow the undergrowth to swallow them whole. But one goal continued to urge Aveline forward.

Many years ago, she had heard whispers of a nearby village, a place of belonging. Her father had silenced the daydreams that followed, reminding her that such tales belonged only to the imagination of a child but she felt drawn to them now and Aveline was certain she would find a place to accept her and Iris. More than anything, she wanted to give her daughter a happy and secure life. And so, she kept walking.

In the distance, Aveline spotted a beautifully intricate twist of thorny branches. Infinitely arched. The hollow center created a tunnel of wood at least 8 feet in height. The branches stood decorated with a colourful arrangement of Starfire Roses, their velvety petals coated with a fine dust that sparkled when the sun hit it just right. Aveline had grown up with stories of The Whispering Veil but few were granted the chance to behold it.

The Veil hummed to her, luring her closer to its grasp. Aveline's intrigue grew as she approached it. She knew she wasn't supposed to enter—The Veil had devoured families before—but the sight of it entranced her and she continued to float mindlessly towards its pull. She hesitated only a moment at its entrance, before stepping inside.

The world disappeared around her. The forest a memory, as she stood surrounded by a blanket of shimmering flowers. Aveline stared into the face of an orange and red rose, inches away from her nose. The flower's sweet smell drifted upwards, hypnotizing her as it reached her nostrils. Her muscles exhaled in relief and the stress melted from her body. Aveline's arms slumped heavily and she looked down at them to see a stranger cradled there. She scrunched her face tightly and tried to recognize the child's young face. The flowers buzzed around her, stealing her focus. Aveline was unable to recall where she had found this child nor how long they had been travelling together. Her body thrummed rhythmically, echoing the Veil's own vibrations.

Her instincts dissolved with its sweet sound, so she placed the stranger on the ground and continued forward.

The Veil sang to her, pulling her deeper and deeper into its grasp. She heard a flurry of voices, all at once, none recognizable but together they created a hushed symphony of murmurs. The voices chanted to her, guiding her towards a future she desperately desired. The promise of safety and warmth. The whispers overpowered her, allowing no space for Aveline's own thoughts to dwell.

It was difficult to make out the words being spoken but one phrase rang through, "Stay with us." An overwhelming feeling of ecstasy overcame Aveline and she twirled gracefully through the tunnel.

It was *safe* here. *Warm.*

She hummed loudly, joining in with the choir, though her own contributions remained unheard against the echoing hush of the others.

This is bliss.

Aveline spun carelessly, taking no notice to her shoulder scraping along the edge of the razored vines surrounding her. Her skin tore away, quickly replaced by the blooming of blood in its absence. The colour captivated her, its warmth spreading down her arm like the comforting glow of a hearth fire. The Veil pulsed around her as Aveline swayed gently, lost in her own stillness—until something cracked through the hush.

A sharp cry. Thin. Urgent.

A baby's desperate plea?
Aveline froze, suspended in time.
Is the cry meant for me?
She paused, allowing it to pierce the silence, digesting the panic beneath it. Behind its desperation, a familiarity shone through. She couldn't quite place it but she knew it called out for her. She turned to the cry, the past returning with each leaden step. The fog began to dissipate from within her. Her mind snapped back to reality.
Iris.
Where is Iris?
Aveline raced through the tunnel, back towards the entrance of the Veil. The whispers shouted out behind her, begging her to stay, all the while Iris's anguished wail carried her away.

Aveline could hear Iris's plea bouncing around her. She knew she was close. Her head darted hysterically, scanning every branch, every nook. She looked up and down and left and right.

And then she saw her.

Vacantly nestled between two thick branches, a sharp thorn pressed against her ice-cold cheek, leaving a bloodless needlepoint prick in its wake. Aveline scooped her up into her arms, begging for forgiveness and ran as fast as her legs would carry her.

How much time had passed within the Veil, Aveline did not know but when mother and daughter emerged, a nearly ripe moon hung low in the sky. Aveline's eyes caught on a flurry of fireflies dancing around the entrance to the Veil. They shone a blazing orange, betraying their otherworldly nature.

Aveline plunged herself further into her river of guilt. She knew to avoid the Veil, yet she had embraced it. She had abandoned her daughter and invited the Fae to feast on their souls.

Frustrated, Aveline chucked a stick at the lights as they buzzed around. It passed through them with ease, their glow flickering only slightly. She screamed at them, squeezing Iris tightly in her arms, though she remembered the whispered stories. These Fae could not follow beyond the Veil.

The Fae responded only with a faint *hiss*, their twinkle fading into the dark, as Aveline hurried away from their lure.

Aveline huffed triumphantly and shifted her gaze to the side. Just beyond the threshold to the Whispering Veil, grew a patch of brilliant green bushes. Aveline recognized the berries growing amongst them, her heart galloping momentarily at the thought of her beloved Bayard. Food had been scarce and delight overcame Aveline as she recalled the succulent taste of her prenatal craving. With a primal eagerness, she ripped a handful of berries from the bush, shoving them into her mouth.

Juice squirted wildly as Aveline chewed. Her smile instantly snuffed out. The berries did not offer the familiar sweetness she had remembered. Rather, they tasted heinous, reminiscent of human flesh with the consistency of bone. Goosebumps prickled Aveline's arms, her delight twisting into disgust. The roof of her mouth pulsed and her cheeks felt as though they had been pierced, vibrating like the buzzing of bees. Aveline spit the berries from her mouth and scrubbed her tongue along her tattered sleeve.

    For a moment, the overwhelming taste was overcome by the fear that these imposter berries may have been toxic. A terrifying dread overtook Aveline as she imagined Iris's life without her. A young girl, all but orphaned, illegitimate in her father's heart. An outcast. Her eyes welled with tears and she nuzzled Iris's forehead. She would not leave her so easily. Not even death would keep them apart.

CHAPTER III

As Aveline and Iris struggled through the trees, she imagined them together in another life. She imagined resting in her marital bed, Iris tucked beneath her arm, while Edrick tended to the animals out front. Ysabel would make them a beautiful stew and mother and daughter would be given the grace to get to know one another without the pressures of exile. Aveline knew she was a good mother but she could never be enough for Iris in a dangerous place like this. She began to weep, the harshness of those thoughts settling in around her.

Through her tears, Aveline saw a flash of golden blonde locks twinkle through the trees. The newly born sun peaked just above the horizon, bringing life to the greenery. A loud noise echoed from the space before her and Aveline caught another glimpse of the mysterious figure. It moved with a determined swiftness—gentle on its feet but fast. Aveline stepped forward, stubbing her toe on a stone, sending it rolling down the slight hill she was perched upon. The apparition froze, whipping itself towards Aveline.

Aveline recognized the long, white nightdress and raised her head to meet Ysabel's kind, doe eyes. Aveline's body throbbed with excitement and adrenaline as she stared at her sister. She called out, eager to embrace her.

Ysabel jumped at the sound of Aveline's voice and took off running. Aveline pursued her clumsily, Iris held firmly to her side. She did not understand why Ysabel would run. Wandering alone in these woods, surely, she had been searching for her. Ysabel continued to flee, dodging branches and thick vines dangling overhead. The forest shouted after her, crunching loudly with the sounds of snapping twigs and splintering trunks. Aveline continued to shout after her but Ysabel refused to listen, hurling herself further into the woods, slowly slipping out of Aveline's sight.

As she rushed past a giant oak, Aveline spotted a torn piece of white fabric trapped between its bark. She stopped running and pulled it free. Raising it to her face, she inhaled the fabric. It smelt of Ysabel.

Several feet away, Ysabel stood barefoot in an open clearing. The light reflected perfectly off her golden hair. Her rosy lips parted slightly as she looked at Aveline with pity. Aveline held Iris high in the air, a sort of white flag with guilty intent. Her sister wouldn't abandon her niece, not again. She stepped towards her slowly, arms raised high and smiled. Ysabel stood frozen, mesmerized in their presence and Aveline took another step. The distance between them was closing and Aveline's stomach twisted with excitement at the thought of their reunion. In this moment, the three of them together was all that mattered.

I cannot lose her again.

Ysabel shook her head suddenly and mouthed an apology as she turned to leave.

Aveline grabbed a large cobble from the ground below her. It was jagged and sharp, heavy as a brick. Without a thought, Aveline hurled the stone towards her sister.

She was desperate to keep her and she would be there to heal her leg's wound. It was a worthy sacrifice for a family's love. But Aveline had never been a good shot and she watched in horror as the rock hit Ysabel in the head, the point of it piercing her temple. Blood poured from the wound and Ysabel's legs buckled beneath. She shrieked and tumbled to the floor.

Aveline ran to her side. Resting Iris on the wet grass, she pulled Ysabel up onto her lap. She was heavier than Aveline recalled but she rocked her back and forth and held her tightly, whispering apologies. Ysabel's chest rose and fell in an unrhythmic fashion as she struggled to keep her eyes from closing.

    Aveline was overcome by guilt. This was not supposed to happen. She slammed her eyes shut, sobbing uncontrollably. Aveline continued to rock her sister, rubbing her fingers through her short, bristled hair. She was terrified to open her eyes, to gaze upon the calamity she had created.

    Aveline pulled her hands downwards, attempting to grasp one of her locks, to twiddle it around her finger like she did when they were children. Unable to collect one, Aveline placed her head on Ysabel's, breathing her in. Her earthy musk filled her nostrils, like mud-drenched leaves. Aveline didn't mind. Many moons had passed from the sisters' last meeting and she was grateful to have her there now. Aveline rested her hand upon Ysabel's coarse cheek and flinched as she let out a loud snort, thrashing her head around in her lap. Reluctantly, Aveline pried one eye open and looked down upon her sister.

    Staring up at her were two dark eyes sitting atop a large snout. Antlers, bigger than any Aveline had ever seen. She shrieked loudly, wiggling her body out from beneath the giant stag. Aveline heard a hundred voices all at once, screaming within the walls of her skull. She scrambled backwards, terrified and confused. She stared at

the deer for a moment, watching it kick its legs wildly, helpless and afraid.
    Aveline's guilt melted away and her thoughts were interrupted by a maniacal laughter. She continued to laugh, her belly growing sore, as she glanced around. With both hands, she pulled a large boulder from the forest floor, plodding her way towards the dying animal. Her arms shook from the weight. She positioned herself above its head and let go. Aveline cackled to herself as she watched the stag's head crush beneath it. Blood sprayed outwards, showering her with its warmth. Aveline bounced up and down on the soles of her feet, giddy and wild-eyed. "Iris, sweetling," she cooed, "breakfast."

    The beast clawed at the ground as Aveline dragged its body along the forest floor. Juggling Iris awkwardly on her hip. She heaved the stag backwards, making little progress and pausing often to admire the antler drawn trenches that celebrated her victory. Aveline's stomach growled viciously, an insensitive reminder to quicken her pace. She puzzled over her next action.
    Iris's icy, pale skin pressed against her side but Aveline had never felt so alone. She started to sob at the realization that nobody was coming for them.
    We will not be saved.
    Slumping down to the ground, Aveline rested her head against the bloodied carcass she

had spent the past several hours towing around. The animal's hair tickled her cheek but its body still gave off a slight warmth which she found comforting in her despair. She allowed herself to rest here a moment, listening to the birds chirp as they flew overhead, before gathering her thoughts and hoisting herself back up to her feet. Aveline wanted nothing more than to hide herself away here but as she contemplated, she reminded herself of the duty she had to her darling Iris.

With a fierce determination, she pulled Iris back up onto her hip. Mumbling a prayer, she gripped the beast's legs before her and continued to pull.

Aveline did not know where they were headed but she trusted the Gods to guide them there. As she lumbered through the endless woods, her faith was all she had to lean on now.

As Aveline's mind wandered, she tried to recall anything that may give her a clue to her location but nothing stood out. Panic began to form within her. The creeping of night loomed near.

Throughout the course of their six-year marriage, Edrick had only brought her to the woods on two occasions. Once on their wedding night and then again four months ago, when it became clear that this pregnancy had stuck. Edrick had presented her with a beautiful bouquet and the two of them had lain together beneath the stars. Aveline had tried to seduce him that night but Edrick had turned her down for fear of hurting their unborn child. She had admired his strength in resisting her after so many celibate months.

    Aveline's body ached as she continued her journey. The dimly lit sky came alive and the evening's first star shone down upon the misplaced trio. They had been travelling all day and Aveline was desperate for a place to rest, when her eyes spotted a familiar refuge. Before them stood their well-worn haven, still intact and inviting them in.

    Aveline ran her fingers up the length of the coarse sticks, settling on the rope tied around the top. She pulled both ends tightly. They didn't move. The sloppy knot had been tied some time ago with steady hands and would not give way easily. Sighing with relief, Aveline smoothed out a spot beneath the branches and cuddling her sweet babe, fell asleep.

    When day broke, Aveline felt a strong sense of determination. Today she would build upon their structure, transforming it into something fit for her young babe. She began by collecting the twigs that lay strewn across the floor surrounding her. Crafting a ring of stones around them, she piled the sticks into a heap. This would be their hearth. A humble flame for both nourishment and warmth.

    Next, Aveline collected some fresh leaves and mud—the shingles of their home and an oversized piece of tree bark—their door. Her final touch, an incongruous bouquet of wildflowers, their mismatched colours and shapes offering comfort and beauty in a sanctuary otherwise void of it. Aveline felt proud of her accomplishment and hopeful for their future. Sitting cross-legged in their new home, Iris sprawled across her lap, she felt shielded and peaceful in this place she had created.

    A thundering crack split the stillness causing Aveline to jump to her feet and peer through the door. There, in the wilderness, stood Edrick. Crackled leaves clung to his shaggy hair. His face was smudged with grime. He wore a sympathetic smile and gestured towards Aveline to join him. Desperate for his touch, Aveline scurried out of the shelter, leaving Iris safely tucked away.

    She approached him, timid but fierce, her thoughts a mix of longing and betrayal. Edrick glanced down at the murdered stag, carelessly lumped nearby with patches of flesh ripped from its carcass and back to Aveline with a saddened regret. He reached towards her and she tumbled eagerly into his arms. Edrick held her for a while, their chests rising and falling in unison, his arms warm and familiar around her.

    "Forgive me," he uttered, his voice shaking slightly. Aveline didn't question his sudden change of heart. Rather, she took him by the hand and led him into the safety of the shelter.

They didn't speak again.

Not when her trembling fingers found the edge of his tunic. Not when their lips met with a desperation she hadn't felt in months. Not even when they clung to each other like the world might vanish around them.

Afterwards, Aveline stared longingly at her husband, her skin drenched with sweat. She had missed the feel of him and the security his arms provided. "Return with me," he pleaded. Aveline felt herself nod in agreement. His hand tightened around hers. "We leave at once."

Edrick led the way while Aveline and Iris marched closely behind. Travelling through these woods with a guard, she was able to notice their hidden beauty. She admired the flowers around them. Beautiful blends of daffodils and tulips, geraniums and marigolds, danced softly in their midst, swaying in the breeze. Aveline lingered a moment to admire their charm, her eyes fixing upon a patch of radiant white lilies. Enchanting and pure. She picked one from its branch and placed it delicately behind Iris's perfect little ear.

She smiled at her radiance, noticing a clump of vibrant red flowers a few steps ahead. Tearing a few from the bush, Aveline rubbed them against her arm, leaving behind a brilliant red. Delighted, she rose the flowers to her cheeks, rubbing them along her cheek bones and then along her lips. She ran her fingers through her thick, matted hair, pulling crinkled leaves from the mess. She did this several more times, growing more aggressive with her pulls, shouting as she tore through her matted strands, frustrated by the state of herself.

When she had finished, her fingers were tangled with thick wisps of dark hair, her head clear of the debris but thinned and patched. Aveline threw back her shoulders, straightened her spine, and scurried off towards Edrick.

Following her husband through the woods, Aveline daydreamed about their first night reunited in their home. He would be delighted by her, a slave to her beauty, as he scooped her up at the old oak door and glided her up the stairs. They would spend hours together, their bodies leading the conversation, while Iris rested in her silk-lined cradle nearby. Aveline could not wait for Edrick to hold her in their marital bed, to finally feel safe again.

They reached the forest's end. Aveline glanced eagerly upon the village. She had lost sight of Edrick during their final trek but her heart fluttered as she imagined him running ahead to prepare for her arrival. She hummed to herself and twirled through the crop fields, each step one closer to her home.

Aveline was surprised to see no lit candles upon her arrival, a gesture Edrick would often welcome her with. She stepped into the entrance way and made her way towards the staircase. The steps creaked in warning, Aveline climbing higher into the grasp of Edrick's lair. A faint light glowed beneath their chamber door as Aveline drew closer to it. She pushed it open, her chest bursting with excitement and locked her sight on Edrick. His eyes were closed but he moaned in ecstasy as she entered.

She inched closer to him, folding Iris into her cradle, tucked tenderly off to the side. She slipped out of her soiled clothing with delicate steps, her feet grazing lightly over the floorboards. The breeze nipped at her breasts, bare and exposed. She placed her hands delicately on the side of their bed, arching her back as she crawled upwards, pulling herself closer to her husband. Edrick moaned again and called out her name but the sound hit her ears differently.

Aveline froze, a timid mouse in bed with a hawk. She felt the presence of another and pulled the covers back daringly, dropping them to the floor around her ankles.

Edrick lay sprawled naked on their bed, his manhood sheathed in the mouth of her younger sister. Aveline gasped as his eyes flung open and he tore Ysabel off him. Ysabel clattered off the side of the bed, grabbing up the blanket and frantically wrapping it around her body. Backing herself into the corner, she slunk away from the light, masking her deception in darkness.

Aveline stood nude facing him and stared at the infidelity before her. Her cheeks were

210

blotched red and chaotic with streaks of pollen smudged throughout. The cracks in her lips were enhanced by the redness she had bestowed upon them. Her hair sparsely covered her sunburnt scalp, her naked body blemished with scrapes and bruises.

"Witch," Edrick thundered. The words slapped her cheeks, stinging beyond any physical contact ever could. "Did I not warn you?"

"Y-you brought me here," Aveline stuttered. "You told me to come."

Edrick scoffed, "Your words assault my ears, Aveline." He rose from the bed shamelessly and pulled Ysabel from the dark. He grabbed at her thigh, tearing the blanket from her grasp and moving her naked body in front of his. "I've replaced your battered old cunt with a younger muse."

Ysabel did not speak. She did not lift her eyes to meet her sister. She stood motionless and unapologetic.

Aveline felt the atmosphere thicken. She struggled to breathe, to even exist in this moment. She stepped back fearfully as Edrick reached towards her and clutched her by the throat. "I did warn you," he growled, squeezing her shoulder with his other hand and heaving her out into the hall.

Aveline shrieked in agony, slapping at his hands, trying to break free. Edrick dragged her into Ysabel's room, shoving her to the floor. He kicked her in the stomach, laughing as her ribs popped from the pressure, before slamming the door behind him. Aveline heard the click of the lock over her sobs. She was trapped. Helpless and shaken, she closed her eyes, calling out to Iris, alone in the other room.

CHAPTER IV

I slunk through the halls of the home that had once belonged to me. The dimming candles suspended on the walls offered little guidance but I knew the way by heart. Silently, I slipped into the bedchamber, Edrick's snores echoing through the home. Hugging the wall, I shuffled over to Iris's cradle and reached down to rescue her. My breath caught at the cold, empty crib.

Where is Iris?

I panicked and set down the stairs. As I crept, I heard an inviting, familiar tune. Approaching the sound, I saw Ysabel floating around *my* kitchen, mixing a bowl of porridge. She sang softly to herself as she worked, tossing a handful of berries into the bowl before focusing her attention on the herb cupboard.

The shelves were fully stocked. Ysabel ventured often to the edges of the forest, collecting a wide array of herbs and spices that grew naturally there. She gathered up a few ingredients and I watched as she added a spoonful of honey and cinnamon and then something more sinister. A pinch of duskroot—a low growing root, flourishing in the shadows and granting its victim an eternal sleep.

Ysabel smiled to herself before speaking. "Sweet sister, I can't return him to you now," she whispered, placing my breakfast on a tray and heading upstairs.

I knew they would be looking for me soon. I had to move fast if I was going to find Iris and rescue us from this dreadful place.

With Ysabel safely out of sight, I dashed for the oak door and threw myself outside. I had no plan. But I knew where I was headed. I ran at full speed, down the crop fields and into the stable.

In my heart, I knew Edrick had brought her here but it failed to soften the blow when I saw her tiny body amongst the hay. I scrambled to Iris's side, scooping her delicately into my arms and began to sob. Iris's body was rigid and ice cold and I knew her final moments had not been spent with love or tenderness.

My hands began to tremble and I kneeled to the ground, the empty place in my chest screaming louder than the wails escaping me.

Iris is dead. And Edrick is to blame.

Tucking her into the corner, I placed a kiss on Iris's forehead, a binding oath that I would return to her. My hands clenched into fists and I stormed out of the stable, leaving Iris *and reasoning* behind.

My march turned to a sprint as the rage in my belly boiled and festered. I ran home, past the towering corn stalks and blueberry bushes, the forest blurring behind me, taunting me to return.

I ran with such a fierceness that even as my foot caught on a gnarled root, I continued to run, hurling my body to the dirt. The ground began to shake around me, splitting sharply and pulling away from itself, a vast chasm left behind in its place.

I am falling.

I clawed at the sides of the pit, loose rocks and soil joining my plunge, failing to slow my descent. I called out into the abyss but nobody heard my cries. The walls stretched infinitely around me. I looked down, unable to see an end to the fall.

I am alone.

Walls of dirt stretched endlessly, reaching up to the sky, the light of it growing smaller the further down I plunged. Against its glow, a figure appeared. She stared down at me, her auburn hair drifting with the wind. Her features familiar, yet not.

I called to her but she did not offer me a reply. She watched me as I fell, studying me with puzzled curiosity. One name whispered through my mind.

Alara.

Aveline woke in a sweat despite the crisp air thrashing against her naked body. She lay curled up on the stone ground, panting wildly and clutching the wall beside her. Glancing around, Aveline noticed that her sister's room had been cleared out in the short time she had been away. The bed and dressing closet had been disposed of, the windows bare. All that remained was the smell of her, a mix of roses and betrayal.

Aveline drew in a long, shaky breath and squeezed her eyes shut briefly before she was jerked to her feet.

She recognized the men, Aldwyn from the neighbouring farm and his younger brother Hugo. Aveline did not know them well but they had always shown her kindness during village feasts and Ysabel held a fondness for Hugo.

At least she had.

Aveline opened her mouth to thank her rescuers but was silenced by a woven sack thrust over her head. She strained to make sense of the men's garbled voices, their hands rough and stout, while they tore her from the room.

One of the brothers whacked her bare backside and heaved her forward. "Move, *witch*," he roared. Aveline could not make out where they were going but she counted their steps as they walked.

Seventeen... Eighteen...

The sun blared hot on her skin, a chatter of voices ringing from every direction as she continued to follow the brothers' lead.

Thirty-one... Thirty-two...

The men's grip tightened on her shoulder.

Thirty-nine...

Aveline's foot fumbled over a damp log and she stepped down into a pool of mud. It oozed between her toes, spilling a thick chill over her nail beds.

Fifty-two...

They stopped.

The sack was torn from Aveline's head, revealing a sloppy pile of sticks and straw. At its center, a wooden post reached eagerly to the kingdom in the sky, while the base of the structure lay littered with holy relics. A trail of salt had been poured with precision, creating a perfect ring around the pyre—a wall of protection from any malevolent evil present there. Aveline turned and found herself surrounded by familiar faces—mothers, fathers, and children too, all staring at her with judgemental and weary eyes.

A watcher shouted from the crowd, "Burn the bloody witch!" The surrounding voices grew louder at the accusation, flooding Aveline's mind with panic and confusion.

Aldwyn and Hugo dug their nails into her flesh and hoisted her up onto the pile.

Aveline did not notice as she was being restrained to the pyre. Her attention was focused on scanning the crowd. Hopeless to find a friendly face, frantically searching for Ysabel's kind eyes or Tessa's reassuring smile. But they were nowhere to be found.

Aveline's eyes began to sting as tears welled behind them. She recognized several faces before her, most scowled and disapproving, while few offered looks of sympathy or understanding masked behind their fear. She darted her eyes back and forth, certainly her sister would not leave her to this fate.

Instead of Ysabel, she saw before her an angel.

My sweet Iris.

Aveline felt a serene hush fall over her body, the Gods had granted her the chance to see her babe one final time before leaving this world behind.

Edrick hushed the crowd and stepped towards Aveline. The chittering behind him stopped as his voice boomed at her. "You stand accused of witchcraft and foul infidelity. For these crimes, you shall burn."

"Husband," Aveline replied, her voice strong and firm. "In life I have loved you true. Do what you must to me but I beg mercy for our Iris.

Raise her well and love her enough for the both of us."

"She is no daughter of mine. Mothered by a whore," Edrick thundered. "She too shall burn." He gestured intently to Hugo and smiled as the flames began their dance.

The fire started slowly, the Gods granting Aveline the grace to look upon Iris's face a while longer, as the flames stretched eagerly towards her, licking her ankles. Her wrists were bound tightly with twisted twine, too thick to be broken by hand. Aveline did not take her eyes from Iris's face as she whispered feverishly to herself.

A concerned villager spoke, "She casts a spell," lobbing a stone in direction with the words. Others followed and stones rained down upon Aveline as the fire journeyed higher up her legs. Her skin began to blister and peel away, like bark torn from a tree. The pain was unrelenting but Aveline did not break her prayer. She continued to fixate on Iris, her mouth muttering the words she had come to know so well.

The blaze climbed upwards, engulfing her waist, her arms, her shoulders. Aveline stood amongst them, a Phoenix begging to be born again.

The licks of heat ignited the twine binding her, devouring it as simply as it had swallowed her body. She wanted to cry out but her faith urged against it and she continued to chant.

The crowd watched as the skin melted away from Aveline's bones. Mothers shielded the eyes of their innocents, fathers demanded they view. Edrick wore a manic smile, his face plastered with satisfaction. He stepped closer to Iris, his arms outstretched.

Aveline finished her prayer and tried to call out to him but the fire had already stripped her of her voice.

Moments passed, fear coursing through Aveline, as the twine disintegrated into a smouldering ash. Aveline felt herself lunge from the pyre. Desperate to save her babe of this cruel fate, she threw herself at Edrick. Drenched in fire, she clawed at his face, the embers lingering upon him.

Edrick screamed out in horror as her hand seared into his flesh, branding him in her memory. He stumbled backwards, clutching at his face and ran, tripping over himself in his panic.

Aveline felt her knees crumble beneath her and fell to the ground just inches from Iris. The smouldered shells of Aveline's lips curled, a mother's smile fighting to bloom.

I have done my duty.

As her body disappeared to ash around her, she stared into Iris's eyes—mother and daughter, together one last time. Aveline shed a final tear, a wisp of steam it's only telling and thanked Iris for being hers.

As her eyelids closed and she welcomed her infinite rest, as the silence crept in, Iris let out a desperate cry.

Ysabel stood alone at the edge of the forest when the screams erupted. She had been foraging chamomile for a night's restful tea when she heard the cries. She sprinted towards the sound to find several of the town's inhabitants shouting wildly.

Oswin the Shepherd towered over the petite silhouette of Iris, a thick log clutched between each fist, intent to strike the babe down.

As her eyes met her sister's burnt corpse, Ysabel launched herself to the front of the crowd, throwing her body protectively over Iris. Oswin faltered, stepping backwards.

"What of this?" Ysabel questioned.

"The child..." Hugo answered. "She... lives."

Ysabel glanced around at the crowd. A mismatched blend of men and women, frightened and confused. Gently grasping Oswin's arms, she lowered the log.

"An omen," she announced, "from the Gods," and scooping the child up into her arms, she headed back home.

When Ysabel entered, Edrick sat moaning in the kitchen. Thora, the village healer, was by his side, tending to the burnt flesh dwelling on his face. He winced in pain as she dabbed it with ointment and tore away the pieces of burnt decay. "My love," Ysabel called, "the child... It lives."

"What news do you carry, woman?" he winced, rising to his feet and leaving behind the piece of mangled skin clutched in Thora's grasp.

Ysabel opened her arms to reveal Iris, pink and plump, cooing lightly. "Your daughter, beloved. Her heart beats."

Astonished, Edrick stepped towards the babe. He reached to her inquisitively, Iris grasping his finger as it entered view. He shook her off and scowled with disapproval. "Have her disposed of," he commanded.

"Sire. She is but a vessel. A calling from the Gods." Edrick scoffed at her words. "Look upon your face," she pleaded, leading him to his reflection in the mirror. Edrick's hand raised to the handprint left upon him during Aveline's final moments, gently caressing the image, before huffing loudly and turning his eyes downwards. "They demand retribution. The balance must be restored."

Edrick struck the wall before him. "And how, *wench*, might you suggest we do that?"

Ysabel flinched at the word. She softened to calm his temper, wrapping her arms tenderly around him. Kissing his *good* cheek she whispered, "A life for a life. You must raise the babe."

CHAPTER V

Iris giggled as her hand bounced from the force of the kick. She rubbed it back and forth, trying to conjure up another, squealing as she felt the pressure of a tiny somersault against her palm. Her long, black hair hung neatly braided past her cheeks as she scrunched up her nose and kissed the swollen belly, her face pushed up against it. "I love you, baby brother," she whispered. She poked at the belly a few more times before looking up. "Mama, how much longer?"

Ysabel smiled down on Iris, "The babe will be here before long, my love," she grinned.

Iris bounced with excitement, spinning happily around the room. From the moment Ysabel had told her the news, Iris had gushed at the thought of becoming a big sister. She had insisted on helping through every step, eager to prove herself useful.

Even now, she settled cross-legged on the floor beside Ysabel who had been delicately folding swaddling bands, miniature nightgowns, and linen caps to keep the baby warm through the winter. Iris grabbed a gown, placing it down gently and folded it in half. She folded it again and again, her pudgy little fingers making a mess of the work, until she held an awkward pile of rumpled cloth. She smiled a nearly toothless grin and passed it off to Ysabel.

Ysabel tucked her under her arm and pulled her close, resting her forehead against Iris's. "Perfectly done, my little lamb. You're settling into your new role quite nicely."

Iris smiled enthusiastically, wiggling her shoulders and puffing her chest, intent on making herself look a little older. The creak of the oak door interrupted their conversation, an announcement that Edrick had returned home from the alehouse.

"Come child, we will need father's help to ready the cradle." Iris's face fell slightly but she rose to her feet and trailed behind.

Edrick stood in the front foyer, swaying rhythmically in place, relieving himself on the floor. Ysabel cleared her throat lightly, "Husband." She curtsied sadly. "Shall I fetch the chamber pot?"

Edrick cackled to himself. "What of it? You'd be wise to earn your keep, woman."

Ysabel looked towards the ground sheepishly as Edrick finished urinating. He grabbed her blouse and shoved her towards the mess. She stumbled, her foot splashing down in the wetness, her legs giving way beneath her.

Edrick's nostrils flared. "Do we live in a barn?" he shouted. "Clean the damn piss! And be quick about it. I'm half-dead with hunger." Iris stepped nimbly to the side, scarcely escaping his wrath as he stomped off.

With Edrick safely out of sight, Iris rushed to Ysabel. She pulled at her arm and Ysabel waddled herself back up onto her feet. Her blouse was soaked with urine and tears streaked her face, Ysabel sniffled and pasted on a smile.

"I'm okay, my love," she whimpered. "Now let's get this mess sorted."

The dinner table was quiet that evening. Edrick slurped back another flagon of ale, paying little mind to the feast his wife had prepared him.

Iris poked her eating knife into her bread bowl repeatedly, fiddling with the handle, her fingers lingering over her initials etched into the wood. The knife was the only gift her father had ever given her, half a year prior. A gift for her fifth name day. Iris sighed to herself, her thoughts returning to the afternoon's events. Her stomach twisted at the image of Ysabel in her soaked blouse.

Looking up from the table, Iris saw a familiar veil of white hair floating past the window. She smiled to herself and requested leave. Edrick hardly noticed her speak, waving his hand dismissively, his beard wet with suds.

Iris beamed and stretched her arms out to Celandine. She felt comforted looking upon her. A girl, just beyond Iris in age. Her nose tilted slightly upwards, angling perfectly towards her shimmering blue eyes. Her ears curled delicately, twisting into gentle points like the tip of a thistle.

Celandine pulled Iris into her grasp, resting her head lightly on her shoulder. Iris's body began to quiver, trapped tears spilling from her eyes. Celandine did not ask her what had happened, likely, she already knew. Instead, she grasped her hand tenderly and led her towards the forest.

Holding onto Celandine, Iris's fears seemed to fade away, evaporating into the wind. Her frown melted to reveal a sweet smile, innocent and free. The two of them sat together, in their usual spot, beneath the cover of a makeshift shelter they had discovered in the woods one afternoon.

Celadine pulled back a vine-laced chair, gesturing for Iris to sit, before tucking her into a shelf of twisted branches. "My lady," she giggled, curtsying whimsically.

Iris snickered, "Why, thank you, *good sir.*"

She poured two cups of berry tea, both girls salivating at the aromatic smell and they continued their role-play. Iris fondly anticipated these stolen moments with Celandine, a chance to escape her homelife and make believe a new reality. She grinned and explored the life of the mask she was wearing.

Today, she was a lady, sixteen years old. She sat surrounded by her seven brothers, staring lovingly into her father's eyes. He spoke to her, his voice calm and reassuring. She did not focus on the words but their tone offered her comfort.

Iris softened further into her chair, taking another sip of her tea. She saw her mother, holding her father's hand, the two of them giggling at each other, eyes full of love and respect for one another.

Another sip. She closed her eyes, eager to see more of this life she desperately craved. The warmth of the tea always had a way of bringing her imagination forward, the images she saw clearer than the real world most of the time.

She turned her head and saw her brother sneak the sourdough from his sibling's plate. He winked at her, whispering a soft *shhhhh*, his puckered lips pressed hard against his pointer.

She chuckled, amused by the younger brother's ignorance and grateful to be included in the game. Looking down, she noticed her own supper, placed tenderly on the wooden trencher before her. She clutched her bread, raising it to her mouth, her eyes adjusting to see a thick, oozing blemish across the bridge of her thumb. She winced at it, turning her hands to reveal more misshapen wounds. Speckled cracks, crusted and dry, flooded her palms. Scarred tissue climbed up her wrists reaching to the elbows.

Iris's delight turned to misery, as it often did at this point of her imagination. She bit into the crusty bread but a metallic, wet taste coated her tongue. She pulled the loaf away to reveal the fluffy white interior, speckled with scarlet. A long, adult tooth jutted out from the bread, its enamel cold and out of place.

Iris brought her hands to her mouth, running her tongue along the empty groove in her gums. It bumped against the tooth beside it, wiggling it gently before releasing it from her jaw. She opened her mouth to speak and the tooth fell free. Her voice caught in her throat.

She realized she did not know what to say. She found herself staring back at this girl's family as more teeth slipped through her blood-stained lips.

The girl's mother rose from the table screaming and ran to her side. Her father trailed just behind and her brothers stayed frozen in place, their faces marked with horror.

Blood poured freely from her lips now. Iris coughed as it overtook the crevices in her mouth, swallowing her oxygen, leaving her gasping.

Iris snapped her eyes open, clutching her chest as she screamed. Celandine offered her an outstretched hand, ready to comfort her friend through the unfortunate ending of her daydream. Iris accepted, clutching firmly to her, her chest thumping loudly and took another sip of the sweet tea.

The village stirred to life, smoke rising lazily from chimneys, as Iris slunk into her homestead. Her father lay crumpled on the hall bench, snoring loudly. She crept past him, her feet sticking to the floor as she snuck through stale ale and shattered glass, abandoned there hours prior. She tiptoed upstairs and down the hall, eager to find her bed but paused when she heard a soft cry emanating from her parent's room.

"Did I wake you, little lamb?" Ysabel called to her.

Iris climbed into her bed, nuzzling up against her mother's touch. Ysabel wrapped her arm tightly around her and Iris noticed a fresh bruise wrapped around her wrist.

"I was troubled by a night terror," Iris lied. She knew her mother would not scold her for her late return home but the lie offered a thoughtful gift—a chance to feel needed after feeling so dispensable.

Ysabel pulled her closer and planted a kiss on her forehead. "Rest now, sweet child," she whispered, stroking her hair. "Mama's here."

When Ysabel and Iris awoke, Edrick had already slipped away. Ysabel prepared the two of them a simple breakfast and, with their bellies full, they headed off to complete the day's duties.

Iris skipped contentedly alongside Ysabel as they walked, her oppressor safely tucked inside the confines of the alehouse.

Ysabel stopped at a baker's stand to admire the fresh smell. Hugo approached, "Good morrow, little miss," he winked at Iris, before fixing his attention on Ysabel. "My lady," he added with a slight bow. "You shine bright this morning."

Iris noticed Ysabel dart her eyes to the floor, a light blush forming on her cheeks. She struggled not to meet his gaze, busying her hands with a meat pie. Hugo reached for the pie beside Ysabel's, his hand grasping lightly at her finger as he moved. He was subtle enough to avoid unwanted attention but Iris noticed and cleared her throat. The noise startled Ysabel and she dropped the pie she had been holding, its contents splattering her and Hugo as he let out a hearty chuckle.

"Blessed be, next week brings my bath. Until then, I shall wear this pie with pride." Ysabel smiled kindly, her eyes fixed still to the baker's stand as Hugo drifted off.

Ysabel scraped the pie she had been holding off the counter, doing her best to wipe away its remnants. The baker had wandered over to them and she handed him enough coin to cover the spoiled pie and a fresh one for the evening's supper. She mumbled a timid *thank you* and headed towards their next stop.

Iris and Ysabel were just about to enter Beatrix's candle shop when Iris spotted Celandine dancing through the market. She spun with a careless freedom, her cheeks dimpled and glowing, each twirl bringing her closer to Iris. "Good 'morrow," Iris grinned.
"And a good 'morrow to you, young lady!" Beatrix boomed in response.
Iris startled, jumping up onto the tips of her toes but smiled up at her and bowed her head slightly. Ysabel gestured for Iris to step inside first but Iris held back, clearing the entrance.
"May I visit with Celandine while you shop?" she asked, grinning innocently at her friend.
Beatrix held a thick purple candle up in the shop window, scents of lilac twisting through the door. Ysabel smiled at Iris and motioned for her to go. Celandine giggled with excitement and the girls took off to a nearby field to play.

The grass tickled Iris's face as they lay together gazing up into the brilliantly blue sky above. The blades swayed gently in the wind, petting her arms, while the clouds danced overhead. Iris and Celandine loved cloud watching, it offered another escape from the world around them. Too often the girls would find themselves laying in grassy fields, marvelling up at the shapes above.

It was in these moments that the friends could confide in each other with anything. It was here Celandine had confessed to Iris that she did not know who her mother was, that Hugo, her father, had made a mockery of some peasant woman after a night of brew. It was here that she had explained that Hugo had not made an honest woman of her but that he had chosen to spare the child the life of a bastard, accepting her into his household. Iris had admired him for this and pitied Celandine for the lack of a mother.

The sun was hot beaming down on them, beads of sweat forming on Iris's forehead. She jumped up on her heels, fanning herself with her hands and ran over to the creek meandering through the valley. The water level was low and spotted with large boulders, their edges worn smooth from years of flowing current. Iris placed her hand into the creek, wiggling her fingers against the stream.

Celandine trailed behind, her shoulders tight and drawn up to her chin. "We should cross it!" Iris declared, a smug smile on her lips.

Celandine crossed her arms, "Father says it's not safe."

"Oh, come on!" Iris teased, stretching her leg out and balancing it on the slick stone closest to her. She wobbled there, lifting her other leg slightly from the edge of the creek, searching for steady footing. She pushed herself off and landed perfectly, throwing her arms triumphantly into the air. "See? It's easy," she beamed.

Celandine puckered her bottom lip and stepped backwards. "I said no, Iris."

Iris's face fell. She grumbled beneath her breath and then hopped to the next stone. Her arms wiggled awkwardly at her sides but she landed on both feet with ease. Celandine squinted her eyes and beckoned for Iris to return. She ignored and sprung further across the water.

Her foot came down on a slimy patch of algae. It slipped out from under her and she fell from the rock.

Celandine gasped and reached out towards Iris who landed on her backside in the middle of the brook. Her clothing was soaked through, streaks of mud tainting the fabric. Iris huffed loudly and then started to laugh, slapping her hands down on the water's surface. It sprayed out around her, misting the plants along the edge. Celandine's hand caught a few of the droplets and she screeched at their touch. She shuddered and shook her hand vigorously, rubbing it against her shirt.

Golden threads flickered along Celandine's wet knuckles, catching the light like a spider's silk.

Probably the sun Iris thought, watching them dance around to her palm.

Celandine snapped her hand behind her back and snarled, "I told you the water is dangerous!" She stomped her feet and stormed off, cradling her hand against her stomach.

"Wait! I'm sorry!" Iris cried, pushing herself from the creek and following closely behind. She had never seen Celandine angry before.

"It's fine," she snorted, her tone betraying her.

Before Iris could respond, Ysabel called out. Iris turned reluctantly and made her way back towards the hum of the village. As she approached, Ysabel sighed, "Sweet child," she scolded, "that's thrice now you've soiled your clothing just this month!" Iris remained silent. "Off to the cloth merchant again, I suppose."

The merchant's shop was bright and inviting, its windows adorned with elegant drapes, rumoured to have come from unexplored lands in far-off places. Beautiful silks cascaded along the walls, cottons folded in tidy piles below.

Walter grinned at Iris, his eyes scanning the damage she had made and led them to a stack of crisp white bolts of fabric tucked neatly into the corner. Walter and Ysabel discussed coin, Ysabel offering a trade in its stead and Iris turned her attention to Walter's young daughter.

She gathered fabrics at the back of the shop, sorting them by colour. Her face displayed a mix of contentment and boredom, her hands working a familiar rhythm. Iris approached her timidly, stumbling into a pile of linen twisted together on the floor. The child shot her eyes upwards before offering Iris a comforting smile. Iris knew of the girl, eleven years of age and betrothed to Lord Eamon. She was gentle and quiet, her dark hair curling perfectly around her sharp features. She gestured to Iris, a silent invitation to join her in her work.

Iris hurried excitedly to her side and grabbed a brilliant blue piece of cotton. She folded it clumsily, Serilda chuckling as she stumbled over her fingers. "Like this," she whispered, placing her hands over Iris's and helping her to fold the fabric. "Father says I must practice if I'm soon to be wed." She grabbed another piece, her hands still atop Iris's and helped her tuck it into shape.

"Do you want to be wed?" Iris asked.

Serilda froze at the question, swallowing heavily. "I am bound to," she replied meekly. "In just three weeks' time. Though the consummation will wait until after I've bled." Iris looked upon her with pity. Serilda seemed to notice, nodding once before returning to her work.

CHAPTER VI

Ysabel stared at the long cloth between her hands as she tightened it around Alys's rounded belly. The cloth, carefully tinged blue with crushed wildflowers, served two purposes—to support the womb leading up to the birth and to entice the Gods into blessing the family with the gift of a son. Ysabel pulled it tightly, crossing it above the shoulders, the fabric slipping slightly from her fingers as the unborn child kicked beneath it.

Alys winced and rubbed her stomach reassuringly, her wrist thin and frail. Her skin stretched tight across her frame, her bones sharp beneath the weight of the womb's sickness.

Ysabel rubbed her arm empathetically, "Have you had your meal?" she questioned.

Alys shook her head, "Can't keep it down," she frowned, returning her focus to her stomach as it bounced with another kick.

Ysabel reached for the small wooden bowl she had prepared, extending it to Alys with both hands. "A tincture of ginger and fennel. Lemongrass too. Picked fresh this morning. It should help to settle the bile."

Alys smiled and raised the bowl to her face, its aroma floating up into the air like steam from a geyser. She parted her lips to take a sip but the scent struck her and she gagged, jerking the bowl away.

Ysabel's eyes softened. She too had faced such sickness in her early days, unable to hold down any feast she had devoured. She had been lucky to overcome it halfway through her pregnancy but Alys had been plagued from the moment she welcomed the child into her belly. "I did bring berries," Ysabel trilled. Alys's grimace lightened.

Ysabel passed her a pouch bursting with plump, purple-hued berries. Alys didn't hesitate. She ripped the pouch open and began shovelling them into her mouth. Ysabel smiled, the berries' sweet smell calling to her as well. She too had grown fond of them through pregnancy, their familiar taste all she could stomach at one point. She resisted their temptation. "I'll gather more on the 'morrow," she said, adjusting the cloth over

Alys's shoulder and then slipping out the front door.

Iris ran to Ysabel as she entered their home, hugging her tightly. She hated being apart but she knew her mother needed to focus when she was tending to those with child. "How is she?" Iris asked, eager to soak up any knowledge she could. Some day she wanted to be just like her mother, kind and tender, doting on the pregnant women of Ravenforge.

"Not eating," Ysabel replied, her nose scrunching involuntarily.

Iris sighed. "Did you bring her the berries?"

Ysabel and Iris had scoured the forest together all morning collecting them for Alys.

"I did," she confirmed.

Iris beamed, "And they were good? Were there enough? Joss won't eat them all, will he?"

"No, little lamb," Ysabel said with a soft chuckle. "Alys's husband is good of heart. He will not rob her of their sanctum. Besides, he finds no pleasure in the taste."

Iris smiled proudly.

"Is Father home?" Ysabel questioned.

Iris puckered her lips and slunk down into her shoulders. She nodded and pointed silently to the ceiling below their bedchamber, bobbing her finger as she furrowed her brows.

Edrick sat at the writing table tucked awkwardly into the corner of the room. He clutched a ratted quill in his left hand, his fingers jumbled and unsure of their positioning and scribbled erratically on the paper before him. He muttered feverishly as he wrote, the words escaping him jumbled and incomprehensible. Edrick looked up as Ysabel and Iris entered the room. The candlelight flickered, bringing life to the shadows licking his fire-warped face—an ode to the ghost that had scarred him so many years ago.

  He slammed his hand down on the table, a cloud of dust billowing out from beneath his palm. Rising from his seat, he held the paper out to Ysabel, a sinister smile resting on his lips.

  Ysabel tucked Iris behind her, sheltering her body from the approaching beast. Edrick chuckled at this, a taunt Iris had come to know well. He crumpled the paper in his hand and flung it at them.

  Ysabel hesitated a moment before taking it. She unfolded it, smoothing out the creases. Her father had taught her to read as a child but the words on the paper were not ones she recognized. Puzzled, she looked at her husband.

  He huffed in exasperation. "The whore's prayer," he growled, as if the remark would answer the questions between them.

  Ysabel stepped closer and put her arms around his waist. She leaned into him, taking the

239

quill from his hand and led him into the embrace. The smell of bitter hops encircled them, its sour taste still dancing on his lips. "Come, love," she whispered. "Perhaps a rest."

    Ysabel raised her lips to meet his, desperate to soothe his temper—hopeful, still, to please the husband that once held her heart. Their lips met and Ysabel sighed at their uneasy comfort. She raised her arm higher up his back, pulling him into her. Exhaling her love into him. Willing him back to her.

    She felt the weight of him shift, his arms stretching out, preparing to draw her in. She smiled to herself, moving in for another kiss but was knocked backwards, her cheek burning with a fiery sting.

    Iris screamed. Her father drew in a slow breath, relishing the moment, before striking Ysabel again. He laughed, striking her over and over, while Iris cried out with each blow, begging him to stop. Ysabel toppled to the floor, her face already blotched purple and blue, her lips torn, splintered and bloody.

    Edrick picked up the paper and dropped it over her. It wafted gently through the air, landing on her chest. "The spell your sister cast that night," he growled. "The curse she chanted while this Devil's brat clawed its way out of her." He spat the words with disgust, staring at Iris through each exaggerated syllable. Saliva clung to the hairs of his beard. His breath was ragged and heavy.

As he yelled, Iris scurried to Ysabel. She huddled timidly by her side, her eyes welled with tears. Tears of fear. Of confusion and hopelessness.

"Your days are numbered," he shouted, his gaze still fixed on Iris. He stomped his feet into the ground, his red, plump cheeks vibrating with the movement, then stormed out of the room without sparing Ysabel a second glance.

Iris helped Ysabel up from the floor. Her arm draped haphazardly over the child's small shoulders, as Iris struggled to keep her steady. They shuffled over to the bed, the floor creaking its sympathies as they moved. Iris guided Ysabel up onto the cold mattress, taking care to lay her gently across it. She climbed up as well, tucking herself beneath her *aunt's* arm and began to sob.

Sleep evaded Iris as she tossed beneath Ysabel. The stolen moments she was able to capture came in fragments, each one fractured by visions of a hideous beast, drunk with rage. Images of Ysabel flashed cowering in the corner while Iris lay there helpless and afraid. A woman flickered through the nightmares, tall and slender, her hair dark as onyx, her body drenched in flames. Iris reached to her, desperate to end her suffering, only to wake briefly before sleep dragged her back and the fire returned.

Iris broke the cycle with a soft cry. "Mother!" though she was no longer sure the name belonged to anyone at all. Its noise stirred Ysabel, who rose with a whimper.

She looked down at Iris, sorrow shimmering behind her eyes. "I'm here," she promised. A lie they both knew. She scooped Iris up in her arms and pulled her onto her lap, wincing at the pressure on her freshly bruised skin. "Should we sneak away?" she asked. Iris replied with an unspoken permission, a sad smile replacing the scowl on her face.

The moon shone brightly in the sky, offering a beacon of hope after the evening's devastation. Iris skipped alongside Ysabel, a reminder that beneath her mature exterior she was still so child-like. Ysabel struggled to keep pace, trailing behind her niece as they walked. Neither one of them spoke, they had no need. Both of them knew where they were headed.

Iris let out a tiny squeal as Hugo's house came into view. She quickened her steps, her excitement overpowering her compassion and hurried off. Ysabel did not mind, she found comfort in knowing that Iris felt safe here.

When Ysabel entered the house, Iris had already disappeared upstairs. Hugo sat cross-legged by the fireplace, his hand patting the floor beside him. Ysabel accepted the invitation and the two of them sat together, watching the smoke billow and rise up the stone chimney.

"What did he do?" Hugo asked, his voice soft, yet concerned. It was uncommon for her to come to him in this way but this time was not the first. She brushed her hair to the front of her face, trying to hide the marks he had gifted her.

"I deserve it."

Hugo stroked Ysabel's hair gently behind her ear. His eyes studied her. Bruises and scars, some new, some old—a battered map of the torment she had endured over the years. "Is that what you believe?" he asked, trying to hide the hurt in his voice.

Ysabel looked up at him, her face painted in shame. "It doesn't matter what I believe," she sighed. "I'm a whore. No better than my sister."

Hugo winced, drawing in a sharp breath, the words smacking him back with the power of fists. He grabbed Ysabel's forearms and pulled her into him. His voice shook, the anger in his words billowing through, "Nobody deserves this, Ysabel. You are not a whore. You are nothing to him but prey." Ysabel stared blankly at him. "Dammit, Ysabel! If you won't protect yourself, I will!" Hugo moved her to the side, his hand firm but gentle. He snatched his coat, the force of it causing the fabric to echo like thunder.

Ysabel gasped. "You can't!" she shrieked, pulling desperately on his arm.

"He is a monster! He won't hurt you again. I'll make sure of it!" Hugo shook her off him, pulling away from her grasp.

Ysabel reached out to him again. "Please! He'll kill you!" she begged, her eyes welled with tears. "Please, Hugo. Please."

"My beloved," he spoke. "I do not wish to see you upset. This man wounds you. He insults you, Ysabel. I would see him harmed and make you mine."

Ysabel stepped backwards, her hand draped over her mouth. She shook her head slowly. "Hugo, I can't... He is my *husband*," she whispered in disbelief.

"The two of you are bound by name, not heart. Let us leave this place, together. Let my love free you." Hugo reached for her, pressing his body against hers. Ysabel surrendered into him, clinging to the words, begging herself to believe them. She moaned as he kissed her neck, not quite in pleasure but in reassurance. Her sound invoked him to continue, kissing her tenderly down her collarbone.

Ysabel pulled back, "Iris?" she questioned.

"Upstairs with Celandine," he winked, undoing her gown and dropping it to the floor. He led her down onto the sheepskin rug placed before the fire. It was soft and comforting against her bare skin. Hugo kissed Ysabel's breast, her swollen stomach, her hip, pausing over each delicate bruise as he wandered. "Lady Hugo," he teased, his lips landing on her inner thigh. Ysabel sighed passionately, her stomach fluttering at the fantasy she was desperately trying to savour.

She wrapped her legs around his shoulders, pulling him into her, as a sudden crash pierced the moment. A child's wail rang out through the sound, causing Ysabel to jump to her feet. Hugo followed to assist her up the stairs, though Ysabel had already slipped her gown back on and raced off.

"Iris!" Ysabel called, the cries growing louder as she approached. "Iris! Are you okay?" She flung the bedroom door open to see Iris sat on the floor atop a bed of broken glass. In her hand, she held the handle of a teapot. She was crying, trying to gather the shattered pieces together, their jagged edges slicing into her delicate skin.

"I'm sorry," she sobbed. "It was an accident!"

"Oh, little lamb. Come. It's alright, dry your tears." Ysabel scooped Iris up into her lap, tearing a piece of fabric from her gown and wrapping it around her injured hand. She looked around the room.

This is the price of my infidelity.

"Celandine and I were having tea," she cried. "We were just having tea. But I saw..." Ysabel shushed her reassuringly. "It was here."

"There, now, child. There is nothing here but us." Ysabel tightened her grip on Iris's hand, crimson seeping through her makeshift bandage.

Celandine floated to her side, tucking her arm around Iris soothingly. "It's okay, Iris," she echoed, nuzzling into her shoulder.

Through the window, the sky bloomed pink and purple as the sun began to wake. Ysabel lifted Iris from the floor. "Let's get you home. That hand will need sewing and your father will soon rise to take his drink."

CHAPTER VII

Edrick was waiting outside when Ysabel and Iris arrived back home. He held his arms firmly across his chest, his face twisted in anger. Iris grabbed Ysabel's hand, the two of them uniting, as they braced for his premeditated impact.

"My love," Ysabel cooed, as they reached the door. "There was trouble at the—"

He scoffed arrogantly and grabbed the back of her head, twisting his fist through her golden hair and shoving her inside. Ysabel winced and exhaled sharply through her clenched teeth, stifling her scream. She stumbled forward, slumping into the table to support herself. Iris clung tightly to her side, their hands still intertwined.

"Papa, truly—"

"Quiet, brat!" he spewed. "I'll not be made a fool after all I've done for the both of you!" Edrick stomped upwards, his nostrils flaring, hands balled up by his sides. He glared intently at Iris, "Don't think your delicate age will protect you," he bellowed, moving closer to her.

Ysabel threw herself protectively around Iris's body, only for Edrick to swat her away with ease, sending her backwards over herself. Edrick raised his fist towards Iris.

Ysabel cried out to them, time slowing around her as Edrick hurled his closed hand at the child she had sworn to protect. Iris clenched her eyes shut, drawing in a sharp breath, bracing herself.

Ysabel lunged at him, the distance between Edrick and Iris closing fast. Crashing awkwardly into his back, Ysabel's small frame bounced off his shoulders. The force was enough to stagger him to the side, his fist swinging down just past Iris's cheek. Edrick huffed, slamming one hand down into the table. As he leaned in to take a second shot, Iris frozen with fear, a knock pounded the door.

Joss shook hysterically, his eyes swollen and red. "Ysabel," he shouted, "the babe…"

Edrick readjusted his posture, his shoulders slumping slightly at the urgency. He cleared his throat, soothing the sting his anger had left upon it.

"Friend," he answered on Ysabel's behalf, his voice kind and unfamiliar, "what has happened?"

If Joss had heard the tussle moments earlier, he made no mention of it. He fell to his knees, sobbing into the palms of his hands. "It's the child," he wept, "my son. Alys needs you."

Edrick reached for his wife, pulling her to his side and placed his hand tenderly on Iris's back. "Come family," he spoke with a practiced kindness.

Edrick, the doting husband of Ravenforge, watched from the shadows as Ysabel kept Alys's gaze and coached her through her breaths of despair. In her lap, she clutched their son, cold and grey. Her chest shook violently as she cried, the baby shaking with its every jolt.

Ysabel listened as Joss explained the quickness of the birth. There had been no time to call for help. He began to weep as he described wrapping their son, silent and unprotesting, in his family's ancestral blanket, before placing him softly on Alys's lap and fleeing to find them.

Tears glistened in Ysabel's eyes, her thoughts on her own unborn son and the pain his loss would plague her with. She found her mind drifting into sympathies for Aveline, who had never been granted the chance to know her sweet daughter. And for every mother that had ever known the pain of losing a child.

She swallowed hard against the lump in her throat as she thought about Bryanna who too had been plagued with The Stillborn Curse, just last week. They had done everything they could to save the babe but just like Alys, it had not been enough. Ravenforge had faced so much loss in the past five years and Ysabel's fragile heart pulsed with the quiet scars of each life taken too soon.

Iris watched the interaction quietly, grateful for her father's momentary peace, yet mournful of the young babe. She shifted in her spot, the movement pulling Ysabel from her thoughts, who in turn called Iris over for assistance. Alys gave the child a final kiss and then tucked him into Iris's arms while Ysabel instructed her to take the babe downstairs and out of sight. Iris obeyed, slipping quietly out of the room.

On the bedside table rested the berries Alys had been gifted the day prior. Hoping to offer distraction, Ysabel plucked one and placed it into Alys's mouth. Alys stared distantly at the wall, hardly noticing as it slipped between her lips. Mindlessly, she began to chew. Ysabel gave her another berry and Alys continued on in her trance, accepting three, four, five more. Her jaw continued to open and close mechanically before the life came back to her eyes and she jerked up in her seat.

Her lip curled and she spat the berries from her mouth, retching all over the bed sheets. Ysabel jumped up off the mattress, turning frantically to search for something to clean the mess but Alys clutched her palm tightly around her wrist. She winced as the force of Alys's hand pushed into the bruises Edrick had left behind the night prior but Alys stared so intently she didn't dare pull away. The colour drained from Alys's face and she began to mutter rapidly under her breath.

Edrick perked up on the other end of the room, tensing his body as he leaned towards the bed. Alys continued to whisper in garbled tongue. Ysabel stared at her in horror, unable to make sense of the situation.

Alys's eyes rolled back in her head, her pupils replaced by cloudy white beads, tracking Edrick's movement behind her. The murmuring stopped, an ominous warning filling their void. "The darkness stalks on thee who waits. Can't hide, can't run." Alys breathed in heavily, her lungs screeching as she finished, "Accept thy fate."

Releasing Ysabel's arm, her body flopped down on the bed. She exhaled loudly and her eyes spun back into their usual position. Confused, she looked around the room, her eyes darting between Ysabel, Edrick, Joss. Her breath shuddered unrhythmically, her limbs twitching at her sides as her head slumped over, deep in sleep.

Nobody spoke of what had happened as they placed the still babe into his forever home—a cedar box no larger than a doll's cradle. His perfect features were an exact image of Joss's and he looked so peaceful Iris thought perhaps he was only asleep. His skin was grey, the dark veins emanating beneath it.

Ysabel shed a tear and placed the lid delicately atop the box. Joss stepped away, unable to control his emotions at the sight of the child. Edrick leaned on Ysabel, rubbing her shoulders empathetically, playing so well the supportive husband's role before his witnesses.

Iris's voice rang out through the silence, "What do we do with him?"

Ysabel squeezed her hand. "We bury him." Edrick nodded in agreement and Joss shuddered a broken cry.

When Edrick returned, his hands were black with dirt. He led them to a shallow grave just beyond the property line and gestured to Ysabel to lay the child to rest. She lifted the box in both hands, taking care not to shake it as she walked and brought the infant to his retreat. The air smelt of fresh dirt and roots and Ysabel trembled as she lowered the box. Scooping Iris into her arms, she turned her away while Edrick completed the task. She took Joss's hand in her own, "If you need anything, anytime," and then bowed her head in sympathy as they left.

Ysabel and Iris started towards home after the incident, while Edrick chose instead to drown himself in tavern ale. Ysabel was thankful for this, grateful for some time to rest and to tend to Iris's earlier injury. They walked home in silence, neither of them able to string together any words worthy of sharing.

Once home, Ysabel brought Iris up to the sewing room where she sanitized and stitched her hand. While she worked, Iris's new dress hung waiting against the wall. Despite the exhaustion, Ysabel found her mind racing.

After tucking Iris into bed, she returned to the sewing room. The dress was long, a little too long for Iris now but it would suit her for many years and the village's fabric came at a steep price. It was porcelain white and Ysabel had taken great care in the stitching. The neckline dipped elegantly and Ysabel knew it would complement Iris's features beautifully, especially as she grew. She held it high in the window, the sun's light reflecting through the fabric and squinted at it judgmentally.

Beautiful as it was, something was missing. She fetched a luscious green thread, stringing it gently through her needle and began to stitch a brilliant design into its hem. Ysabel extended the stems along the length of the gown, pairing them with bold purples and pinks—Iris's most favourite of colours. Once she had finished, she smiled to herself. Ysabel had been working on it for months but finally, it was complete and just in time for Iris to boast it at Serilda's upcoming wedding. She sighed gleefully to herself and finally slipped away to her bed.

The bedchamber walls shook forcefully with the slam of the door below. Ysabel jolted upright. The dark sky kept the night's hour secret. She rubbed her eyes as the walls shuddered again, shaking with each booming step rising up the staircase. The door burst open and Edrick stormed in.

"This village is a curse," he growled with an unsettling calmness.

Ysabel stared blankly, yawning and stretching her arms out.

"I saw Branric at the alehouse," he continued. "He's been there often since Bryanna lost their babe."

Ysabel straightened in the bed.

"Thing is," Edrick muttered, pacing the room, "he's been talking. And it's got me thinking." He sat beside her. "It's the berries, isn't it?"

Ysabel cocked her head to the side, placing a gentle hand on his shoulder. He shrugged her off. "Because all those lost babes, every last one, had something in common. You know what that is, don't you, Ysabel?"

She opened her mouth to reject but no words came through. Edrick laughed coldly, "Nothing to say for yourself?"

Ysabel sat up straighter, blinking hard. "I don't—" she began.

"—have the spine to speak it aloud!" he spat. "You never have. But *I* can see it now."

She reached for him again, her voice soft and pleading. "My love... the drink has overtaken you."

"Enough!" he roared. "Do I look like a donkey-brained fool?"

Ysabel blinked slowly.

"All these years," he shouted, rising to his feet. "I should have ended it. I should have known the curse ran in *your* blood too." His voice dropped to a murmur. "Should've seen it sooner."

Ysabel rose slowly, arms outstretched. The back of his hand caught her cheek with a sickening crack, sending her to the floor.

"Enough of your fucking lies!" he bellowed, his voice desperate and unforgiving. "Bryanna. Alys. Even Aveline loved those damned berries. Gods know how many more."

The anger in Edrick's voice was new. Wrathful.

Ysabel perched herself up onto her forearms and was met with a debilitating blow, knocking her back down to the floor.

"Please. You're not making any sense," she whispered but Edrick could not hear her voice over the chaos of his mind.

He hit her with a forceful kick, her ribs shattering under his boot. She reached out towards the door, digging her fingertips into the cold stone, clawing her way to freedom.

As her body dragged along behind her, she tried to reason with the demon, begging Edrick to let her go. He only chuckled, hoisting her briefly off the ground before hurling her out into the hallway and down the stairs.

"I should have seen it sooner." He grabbed the back of her gown, yanking her by the fabric and forcing her eyes to meet his. "But I guess, it was always going to end this way, wasn't it? The Gods have been testing me," he sneered. With a cruel laugh, he lunged her towards the hearth. "Accept thy fate, Ysabel."

She screamed as its warmth teased her face. She inhaled sharply, attempting to distance herself from the flames but her bones lay broken and helpless.

A tear welled, falling unnoticed, as Ysabel cupped her swollen belly and the babe beneath it. She opened her mouth, a final bargain for her life *and his* but her breath fell silent.

Edrick towered over her, flushed and sweaty. He wobbled in place. "No spells?" he chuckled, wrapping his fat fingers through her golden locks and forcing her into the starving fire. "Your Devils can't save you now."

The smell of singed hair filled the room as Ysabel's face bubbled and blistered amongst the flames. She kicked wildly, grabbing at Edrick's hands. He cackled through her screams, the sound lingering beyond the silence that accompanied her body slinking lifelessly to the floor. The kicking and squirming ended and Edrick pulled Ysabel's scorned body from the fireplace, tossing her mercilessly to the side.

Iris hid beneath her covers when the screaming erupted. Her father's voice barked louder than any she had ever known and just the sound of it was enough to frighten her.

Throughout Iris's entire life, she had only seen Edrick smile three times. None had been for her. Iris often found herself daydreaming about the man her father used to be, the one Ysabel painted in her stories. On many occasions, she told Iris of the kind and gentle man who had won her heart. Iris rolled her eyes.

That man isn't here.

Ysabel screamed louder, the cry echoed by the sound of something tumbling down the stairs. Iris winced. She sprung out of her bed and stomped towards the door. She could be brave. She would put a stop to this and teach her father never to mess with them again.

"Your Devils can't save you now," he roared from the sitting room.

The malice in his voice sent Iris racing back to her bed. Her body thumped with each beat of her heart, her breath shuddering loudly around her. Almost loud enough to drown away Ysabel's shrieks.

Iris began to weep for her aunt, the only mother she'd ever known, the guilt of her paralysis gnawing at her soul. She waited patiently for the screaming to stop, for her father to grow thirsty or bored and leave her be. The second he was gone, Iris would be at Ysabel's side to mend her wounds and to comfort her. This was always the way but Iris knew with each beating that someday soon she would have the courage to face him.

Edrick's laughter bellowed through the house as the screaming came to an end.

Iris took a deep breath and counted to herself.

One... Two... Three...

At twenty, she peeled back her covers and crept to her door. She tiptoed down the stairs and peered cautiously around the corner.

Edrick did not hear her approach. He was crouched to the ground, his back obstructing Ysabel from view. Her head poked out beyond his side, the skin black and charred. Her scalp was nearly bald, with small patches of hair still smouldering against it.

Iris caught the gasp in her throat. She wanted desperately to run but she could not take her eyes off her aunt's scarcely recognizable face. The flesh had burnt away to reveal fragments of exposed bone, framing the scream still caught on Ysabel's jaw.

Iris stared for a lifetime, Edrick unaware of her watchful eyes as he shook Ysabel vigorously. She watched his arms jerk back and forth, her vision always drifting back to find her aunt's mangled face silently shouting out to her. Her eyes lay vacant, the lids burnt and gone, howling out a grimacing tale.

Iris's gaze was interrupted by the shrill *ting* of the butcher's knife crashing to the floor. Edrick backed away from the body, his arms stained to the elbows with blood. He cradled something against his chest but Iris could not make out what it was.

She jumped back fearfully and Edrick looked her up and down with a crazed stare. He smirked, unbothered by the interruption. He laughed, "Look what dear Ysabel has cursed us with."

Iris gaped at him, unable to respond or make sense of the horror she had stumbled upon. She glanced down at her aunt's body, the entirety of it now within her view. Her stomach had been sliced jagged, the fat pulled back to reveal an empty womb. From the wound, the umbilical cord twisted up into Edrick's arms, still attached to the babe he was clutching, tethering life to death.

"You really should thank me," he sighed, "I've ridded us, finally, of this house's evil." His eyes flickered down to Ysabel's corpse, "Unless you disagree? Careful girl, wouldn't want you following your kin down to hell," he chuckled, kicking Ysabel's side one final time.

Several days passed before Iris's bravery grew large enough to lead her to visit her aunt's body. The stench of her filled the entire home but it was much stronger as Iris stood before the fireplace.

Edrick had spent the past days in his cup and nobody had been by to check on the family. Surely, Hugo and Celandine at least would have noticed their absence but they too kept their distance, despite Iris's many prayers.

She whimpered as she stared down at Ysabel's defiled corpse, the scent of it twirling her stomach. In the corner, her baby brother lay still and grey, his glassy eyes stuck upon his decomposing mother. Iris strode over to him, scooping him up into her arms. She would grant him a proper burial first and then her aunt.

Tucking him tight into her chest, she turned for the door, her father's voice slicing the silence. "Leave him, girl," he ordered, "his work's not yet done." Iris jumped at the intrusion, the babe bouncing in her grip.

She grimaced. "Father, he's not breathing. He deserves to rest."

Edrick only laughed. "He needs time. Her Devils will revive him."

Iris squinted at him, her heart racing fiercely in her chest. "I don't understand—" she stammered.

"Neither do I," he admitted. "But they all..." He faltered, then began again. This time speaking not to her but to the storm unravelling in his mind.

Amongst them, Iris heard their names—*Alys, Bryanna, Aveline.*

Feeling brave, she interjected, "Alys and Joss buried *their* son."

"A fool's act, indeed. The child stood a chance before the earth swallowed him."

"Father," Iris pleaded, ignoring his drunken babble, "Your dislike of me is no secret but please, let me bury them."

"I do not dislike you, Iris. *I see you.*" Edrick softened, shuffling anxiously, a sight Iris had never witnessed. "You too entered this world silent and grey. The curse awoke you, as it will your brother." He trailed off, shifting his thoughts inwards. "The berries stain the soul. They mark the damned. The berries..." He began to tremble, the phrase looping, interrupted only by sporadic laughter bursting from his throat.

Iris placed the baby delicately back on the floor. Edrick continued to ramble to himself, taking no notice as Iris clutched Ysabel's arm and dragged her towards the door. Granting her aunt a peaceful rest was the least she could do as retribution for the sins she had endured.

With all of her strength, she pulled her towards the forest, Edrick's voice growing quieter with each faltered step.

When they reached the woods, Iris felt a tremendous relief wash over her. She spotted a nearby patch of dirt and began to dig. Having not had time to plan the burial, she had no shovel to aid. She threw herself down on all fours and clawed furiously at the soft soil beneath her.

The sun was setting on the horizon as Iris completed the hole. Her mouth was dry and her fingers ached as blood pooled beneath the nail beds. She wiped her brow, smearing the musk across her forehead.

Grabbing Ysabel, she shuffled her into the freshly dug grave. Iris scooped the loose dirt surrounding it, watching intently as her aunt's face disappeared. She cried only momentarily before rising to her feet. She had been forever changed.

Bowing her head, Iris whispered a gentle prayer. She rubbed her hands on her white dress—the one Ysabel had finished sewing only hours before her heinous murder. The dirt stained the fabric, as Ysabel had stained her heart.

She smiled sadly at the beauty of it, pulling at the sides of the gown, watching as they danced elegantly in the wind. Iris knew she would forever treasure this final gift to her. In fact, she may never wear another gown again.

She looked down upon the radiant stitching along the dress's hem, admiring each meaningful weave. Her heart warmed as she cherished it, the purples and pinks atop the bright green thread.

She inhaled deeply, memorizing this moment and focused only on the uniquely patterned lilies her *mother* had created for her.

PART THREE

Chapter Sixteen

Lily sways gently, her attention focused on Alara and Bram. Her feet, bare and oozing, are planted in a river of blood trailing to Auryn's shredded corpse. Alara steps towards her and she flinches at the sound, lunging her shoulders in their direction. She stumbles through the puddle, the hem of her dress skimming along Auryn's bloodied remains, painting over the once vibrant purple and pink lilies stitched there. Their image becomes a memory.

  Alara shakes her head vigorously, knocking herself from her daze. She stares unblinking at Auryn and startles at the sound of her own scream tearing from her throat. She runs to his side and pulls him up into her lap, his arms dangling lifelessly. She rakes at the ground around them, pulling in the bits of him Lily had torn away and squishes them into Auryn's body.

"Fuck," she sobs, blood and flesh slipping through her fingers. Alara whispers incantations from memory, pulling the words directly from Serilda's old journals. She mutters spells of restoration, of anchoring the soul, spells of healing. Auryn continues to lay still and unmoving, blood flowing from the gaping hole in his throat.

Lily stares at them with milky eyes. Her lips are stained with Auryn's blood and her mouth opens and closes as she dances in place. Chunks of tissue fall through the gape surrounding her jaw. She doesn't even seem to notice.

Alara lays Auryn gently on the ground and stomps to her. "You fucking killed him!" she cries. Lily doesn't react. Alara leans forward and pushes her back. Lily snaps in her direction, leaping at Alara. She jumps to the side and dodges the attack.

Bram moves in behind her on the defence. He raises his blade and plants his feet firmly into the ground. Alara doesn't turn but she hears him and raises her hand, stopping his counter.

"No," she breathes, "I'll handle this."

"Auryn is dead," Bram snaps, "this isn't the time for sentiment or mercy. Let me end this." Without waiting for an answer, he pounces forward. Alara responds swiftly, knocking him onto his ass.

"Auryn was my friend..." she whispers bleakly. She glances between the two of them and shudders. "Lily will get her end. On *my* terms."

Bram rises back to his feet and rubs his lower back. "Don't let her bite you too," he growls.

Alara steps closer to Lily who snarls as the distance closes between them. Lily reaches out to her, teeth bared and stumbles forward. Her knees buckle and she collapses to the ground. She thrashes her arms wildly, shaking her head back and forth, trying to wiggle herself up. Alara looks back at Bram with sorry eyes.

Lily continues to growl and twist at their feet, swinging her arms out to the sides, slapping herself in the cheek. The impact stuns her for a moment, calming her enough for Alara to boost her back up into a standing position.

"I'll get her out of here," Alara mutters bleakly. She reaches out and takes Lily's hand, the way she always has.

Lily's shoulders relax and she falls in line, shuffling clumsily behind Alara as she leads her away.

Bram snorts behind them, "So, should I just wait here for you then?" he questions meandering over to a thick log nestled in an overgrown patch of vines and shrubs. Alara doesn't respond. "You know he's my friend too," he calls after them.

Alara continues on, unable to look back to Bram, refusing to look at Auryn's mangled face and accept the tragedy. She clutches Lily's bony hand in hers and marches through the trees. She ducks to avoid a large branch in her path, pulling it slightly to the side as she manoeuvrers through. The branch springs back and smacks Lily in the side of her head. She doesn't flinch as the tree's thorny claws tear the decaying skin from her forehead but she does stop walking. Alara tugs at her arm but the girl refuses to move.

Alara grumbles to herself and steps behind her. She poises her arms on Lily's back and shoves her forward. Lily snaps her head around and pounces at Alara.

She jumps back as Lily clamps her jaws shut, inches away from Alara's throat. Alara draws the blade from her hip and slices the space between them. A warning Lily couldn't possibly comprehend. Instead, she leaps at her again and Alara slips to the side, dancing around her and back onto the path.

"This is how you want to do it?" she screams. "Fine!" Alara stomps off. Lily follows.

She keeps a slow pace, allowing just enough distance for her to stay ahead of Lily without the risk of her trailing off. Lily continues to pursue her, growling every once in a while. A reminder that her hollow husk has shifted into something twisted.

Alara sighs to herself, thinking of all the times Lily had been a friend. The comfort she had given Alara. She turns back to face her as they walk. Lily stumbles amongst the trees, knocking into more obstacles than she manages to dodge. Her skin oozes, the foul smell filling the air. Yet, in the silent moments, Alara can still see the girl she has come to love. "How have you become this?"

Up ahead, Alara spots Lily's shelter. As they approach it, she feels a heaviness in her heart.

This wasn't supposed to happen.

Lily lingers behind her, her limbs jerking unnaturally, arms outstretched.

Alara stops at the entry way. It is shrouded by a fresh overgrowth of Soulshade Berries. For a moment, Alara is puzzled by their existence. It's been some time since she has seen the icy purple beads, since she has smelt their rancid perfume. The thought passes quickly, replaced by the churning of her stomach. The berries shouldn't grow this close to the village. The Ancestors had been sure of that many years ago. So many had been lost to the forest.

Lily continues to make her way to Alara, quickening her pace as she grows closer to home. Alara raises her blade and aims it for Lily's heart. She braces herself, waiting for Lily to close the gap and end the suffering. Her left ankle has snapped on the journey but it doesn't stop Lily from sprinting towards her. Alara plants her feet firmly into the ground and locks her eyes on the target. "I'm sorry," she mouths—just as Lily curves to the side and hurls herself into the berry bush.

Alara's shoulders fall, the tension leaving her body. She walks over to Lily with an undeserved relief. Lily is crouched in front of the berries, sniffing them animalistically. She nudges the bush with her nose and several frozen berries drop to the ground. Alara shivers as she imagines Alec getting his hands on their poison. The Ancestors had burned them for good reason. To end the cycle of the falsely stillborn and to shield their souls from the hungry Fae.

Alara searches her surroundings, her eyes settling on the frayed bit of twine at the tip of Lily's shelter. She tears it free and the sticks collapse into a tangled heap. Lily turns fast as they clatter to the ground and Alara feels a flicker of remorse. She kicks the loose branches over to the berries and strikes her dagger on a nearby boulder. It sparks and she strikes it again, pressing the twine against it. The flame doesn't hesitate. It swallows the parched rope, engulfing it so quickly Alara burns her finger before tossing it against the berry bush. She breathes in sharply and mumbles a prayer.

Please ignite.

The twine sizzles out, the heap of sticks beneath it unscathed. Alara curses under her breath, defeated by the cursed berries. She lunges forward at the bush, dagger in hand, screaming and hacking away at them.

The berries fight back, their sharp thorns slicing at Alara's wrists and arms. She doesn't stop. She releases a primal wail, throwing herself deeper into the shrubbery, welcoming each shallow scratch. She grits through the pain, squeezing a thick bunch of berries together and slashes through several crimson stems.

For Auryn.

She yells and stabs at another low hanging branch.

For Lily.

She swings again, her dagger knocking from her grasp. It lands somewhere behind her but she does not try to retrieve it. Instead, she throws herself into the shrubbery. Alara balls her hands into fists and punches the thicket. The fruit damages her more than she does it but she kicks and pulls, stomps and shreds. Her face pours a warm clear liquid—sweat or tears—Alara does not know. And still, she does not stop.

Beside her, Lily tilts her head inquisitively, her own internal rage evaporated. She doesn't react to Alara's outburst, she only stares in her direction. Alara's arms seep blood, thousands of knicks, like frost-kissed glass. She surrenders to their painful sting, grateful for the distraction from the pain in her heart, as she again springs forward.

A loud popping sound erupts from the bush. It pierces the sky, cracking like thunder and is followed by another. In quick succession, the berries continue to shatter, their icy exterior snapping away in brittle shards.

Alara steps backwards, mesmerized, as a low flame flickers from inside the thicket. It travels along twisted stems, bursting each berry along its path, igniting from within. The fire spreads quickly, engulfing the bush in seconds. Molten thorns glow hot and embers rain down from the sky. Lily stumbles closer to Alara and rests her head softly on her shoulder.

Just like old times.

Alara looks down at her with sympathy.

Whoever you are, I hope you were loved.

She runs a hand through her matted hair, thick strands clinging to her fingertips long past their touch. "You didn't deserve this life." She takes a deep breath, summoning all of her strength and pushes Lily into the flames.

Lily stumbles within them, tumbling into an outstretched branch. It pierces through her stomach. Lily doesn't wince, she doesn't cry. Instead, she stands tall amongst the flames, arms outstretched to Alara.

Alara blinks hard, fighting back the tears taunting her behind her irises. She reaches back to Lily reassuringly and watches as the thinned hair on her scalp ignites. The flames spread down the nape of her neck, sparking her dress, travelling down to her feet nestled in the soft ground below her. As the fire overcomes her face, Alara notices her head shift to the shelter she had known all these years. Lily leans towards it, her skin flaking away, floating with the embers on the breeze. She turns her head back to Alara and smiles, before buckling to the ground and disappearing into the flames.

Alara clutches her stomach and glares into the fire. Her heart pounds heavily in her chest. In less than an hour, she has lost the only two friends she'd ever known. Her shoulders shake as she sobs and shouts out into the forest's abyss.

The thicket crumbles to ash, sparing nothing. Alara presses her palms against her cheeks, wiping them clean. She straightens her back and takes a deep breath of composure.

Bram needs her and Auryn deserves a proper rest. She shakes her head clear and starts back towards them, willing herself forward. Step by painful step.

Chapter Seventeen

"I don't think I can take much more of this," Bram breathes. Behind him he drags a net of vines, the rough weaves uneven and hasty, betraying the rush of its creation in Alara's absence.

Auryn's body lies strewn across it. Bram grunts as the net catches on a root, tearing the bottom edge away.

"Fuck," Bram curses. "This isn't going to hold."

"It has to," Alara answers, her eyes avoiding Auryn's corpse as she grabs at the end that gave way.

"Why?" he chokes. "What's the point? We're not saving anyone. People keep dying no matter what we do."

"No," she snaps. "We can't afford to think that way. Ravenforge depends on us. No matter how we feel about it."

Bram shakes his head. "This forest won't stop taking from us. Now we have to worry about the Scabs, too?"

Alara's mind drifts to the faces of those lost over the past decade.

She remembers her mother. Not the way she lived but her vulnerability when Alara found her half-buried in the middle of the woods. She remembers the mud on her hands as she dug her free from the earth that had tried to devour her. She had sung to her as she dragged her mother's body through the forest, until her throat stung raw. As if the sound could lead them home.

Her heart thumps at the memory of Auryn's parents. Such little time passed between their ceremony and her mother's.

She remembers Isaac. His wide smile and the way he had always called her *Miss Alara*. He'd looked up to her. He'd trusted her in the same way Alec once did. She was supposed to keep him safe. She was to be his mentor the following year.

Melinda. The way she'd screamed in the fields when she saw her bloodied little boy in Alara's arms. How her corpse wore that same scream in death.

And Auryn... His name settles in her chest like a stone. He wasn't supposed to break down her walls. He wasn't supposed to get in. She

remembers his laughter. It was warm, soothing. The way he looked at her. Like he *saw* her. The weight she carried. The prickly edges she'd grown.
Lily.
"I'm such an idiot."
Bram looks up at her. "The Scabs have been here for hundreds of years. Before our grandparents and their parents too. They've never attacked anyone before. We couldn't have known—"
Alara turns away from him, hiding the tears brimming her eyes.
"That Fae had my mother's face," Bram whispers. "It spoke in her voice..."
Alara doesn't answer.
"What does that mean?" he pushes. "She's just started getting better. She hasn't been in these woods. It couldn't have harvested her."
"Bram—" Alara shifts back to face him, dropping the net from her hands. "We've all heard the tales."
"No," he insists. "It's not possible. She can barely walk ten feet on her own."
Alara sighs. "The Swarm can't wear her skin unless they've tasted her soul's essence."
Bram swallows hard. "Let's just get back to them."
Alara nods, pulling the net back up into her hands. After all that has happened, she's eager to reach the village and find Alec. She imagines sipping stew with him and Deia, safely away from

the forest. Together, they'll grieve Auryn. The village united... He'll receive the hunter's burial he is entitled to and the village will keep breathing, as it always has.

In the distance, black smoke billows over the treetops. Ravens circle above, their dance choreographed and familiar. Bram and Alara share an uneasy look, quickening their pace.

The forest is quiet, its wildlife hidden from sight. An eerie charge echoes through the air, raising small bumps along Alara's arms.

Something is wrong.

Both hunters sense it, their strides bursting into a run. Auryn rattles behind them, the undergrowth crashing into him as the vines begin to tear away from themselves.

They reach the clearing. Something lies in the tall grass, where the trees begin to thin. A knitted shawl sways from a low hanging low branch.

Bram drops to his knees, wrapping his arms around his face. He pulls at the hair on the back of his head. He sobs violently and chokes out the word, "Mum..."

Louisa's body is twisted and discarded at the base of an ancient oak. Her dress is blood-soaked, the fabric on the left side torn and clinging around the jagged wound just beneath her shoulder. Her face is split from mouth to ear, the flesh peeled open and left dangling as though something had tried to unzip her skin. The horror

Bram had seen hours prior lies before him now, the Fae's glamour taunting him still. He stares at her, unblinking, tears flooding from his eyes.

Alara steps towards her. She lifts her body and places her beside Auryn on the net. She grabs the edge, pulling tightly. They do not move.

"Bram," her voice is firm. "We have to go."

He doesn't answer her. He remains on his knees, eyes locked forward. No sound surfaces. Just a wide, frozen stare, his world torn away.

She crouches, grabbing his face with bloody hands, forcing him to meet her eyes. "We need to move. Now." Something flickers in him. He nods, barely and staggers to his feet.

They march forward in silence, the unknown overtaking their minds. Alara reaches out to him, laying a shaky hand on his arm. Knowing that nothing she can say will help yet reassuring him she is there.

By the time they reach the village, thick smoke hangs low, casting Ravenforge in a haze of black and red. The fence has been torn away. The wooden posts scatter the field.

Alara slows. The path beyond is littered with debris and ash—scorched wood, shreds of clothing, the shattered remains of carts and barrels.

She shifts her grip on the net, wrapping the loose ends tightly around her fist. Bram struggles at her side, his expression blank. His body trembles with the weight they carry behind them, the carnage that lies ahead.

The village is unrecognizable. A pile of ruins, blanketed with the debris of collapsed buildings and rubble. The air carries the scent of soot and charred meat, thick enough to taste.

A faint buzzing cuts through the stillness. It rises as they move to the main road of the village.

Flies.

A sea of them. There are so many the hunters are forced to drop the net and swat them away. They coat the ground in a black wiggling frenzy. Alara steps onto the road, disrupting their feast. They scatter, unveiling the butchery that hides beneath.

A severed leg.

A child's arm?

Alara blinks, her heart stopping. In the upturned palm rests a small wooden sword. Tiny fingers curl around the hilt, refusing to let go.

Her stomach twists.

The darkness of the forest is more inviting than this. The monsters that lurk there feel more real. Alara wants nothing more than to run back there, to run back in time and smother herself in the cruelty of the shadows. Yet the unknown carries her forward.

She takes another step. And another. More flies erupt beneath her boots, revealing broken limbs and a severed torso, its jaws stretched open in a chilling scream. The chest cavity has been torn open, exposing ribs and missing organs.

    Bram scoops up his mother's corpse, pulling her into an embrace, resting her head against his shoulder and walks forward. The flies buzz around him as he continues to their cottage, carefully stepping over the cluttered pieces of his people, dodging the slaughter in a hazy numbness. Alara stands in place, her legs stiffened with the tragedy, the village blurring around her.

    Bram's boot stumbles over the threshold of the door, Louisa's body shuddering in his arms as he struggles to keep his grip around her waist. He moves carefully through the remains of their home. The walls have crumpled along the edges, the wood blistered and smouldering. The cottage's frame is all that stands between them and the charred village outside.

    Bram moves carefully through the remains of their home, Louisa cradled tightly in his arms. Broken furniture lies strewn across the splintered floorboards. His childhood echoes faintly in the wreckage. His mother's voice, the warmth of bread and story time. The creak of the rocking chair she'd always favoured, now reduced to soot and legs.

    Bram carries her towards her bedroom, shuffling his feet through thick cinders that coat the floor around them. He whimpers at the sight of her bed, somehow untouched by the chaos, the shape of Louisa still imprinted in the mattress. He brushes the bed free of ash and rests her upon it. He fluffs the bedding around her, pulling the blankets up under her chin, just as he had the night before.

Glancing around the room he notices a flicker of brass peeking slightly above the debris. His mother's bell. He takes a deep breath and walks over to it, pulling it upwards. It resists, buried beneath the scraps of the room's furniture. He tugs harder, kicking away the remnants of Louisa's end table with his foot. It comes loose and Bram stumbles backwards with it, landing flat on the ground.

A frail hand squeezes the handle, the skin scorched and grey. He traces his eyes along it, down the palm and past the wrist, up to the shoulder. He recognizes each mark and freckle. So many nights he had spent holding this arm, comforting his mother through her sickness.

Bile creeps up his throat. He stares unmoving, his breath lodged.

She had been calling for him.

He carries it back to the bed. His knees nearly give out from under him as the room shifts through his vision. He regains his balance, placing her arm beside her, prying the bell from her grasp before tucking the blanket firmly at her sides, hiding the mess beneath it. He slips the bell into his pocket.

"I'm sorry, Mum," he whispers, kissing her gently on the forehead. "I should have been here."

Chapter Eighteen

Alara stares down at Auryn's body, still wrapped in the net of vines.

She swallows against the lump in her throat as she looks between him and the slaughter around her. Her gaze lifts slowly, drawn upwards against her will, to the bleeding sky.

This isn't real.

She slows her breath, listening for Alec's familiar cry, the assurance that this is all another nightmare.

The village is silent.

"Alec!" she shouts.

Nothing.

She stumbles to a black, soot-stained wall, her breath unravelling, coming in shallow bursts.

The sky warps on the horizon. Clouds roll outwards in all shades of orange and red.
Wake up.
She yanks her dagger free from its sheath, nearly dropping it in her haste. She pushes her sleeve away from her forearm, skin bare and waiting. She doesn't hesitate. She drags the blade across her arm, sharp and quick. She hisses as blood and pain flash beneath the steel.
I'm not dreaming.
She squeezes her eyes shut. When she opens them, the sky is still burning. Auryn is still dead.
Ravenforge has fallen.
Alara sheathes her blade and stumbles down the main road, her eyes locked on Deia's cottage. Her vision doubles as she moves forward. She trips over a severed leg and falls, her chin recoiling off Deia's doorway. Her eyes land on one of Alec's carvings, tenderly etched into the corner of the second step. A protection rune. One of the first he had learned just before their mother's passing. He had snuck out one morning and chiselled it there while the village slept. Deia had found it at dawn, his jam-smeared dagger left carelessly behind. She had scolded him for days but Alara always noticed the way her lips curled into the hint of a smile when she spoke of it.
    Alara pulls herself from the memory, looking up to the door. It hangs open. There's no scent of fresh bread. No enticing aroma of pastries

or stew. The air pulses with the stench of flesh and bones and the tickle of flies swarming around her. She pushes up off the ground and forces herself up the steps. She shoves the door open further and wills herself to look inside.

The cottage draws her in with the warm invitation it always has. A low fire burns in the center of the room. The home stands tall and familiar, a stark contrast against the destruction and death beyond its doors. Alara inhales deeply. She scans the room.

It speaks its own tale, betraying its peace with the signs of a struggle. The walls, unspoiled by fire, are splattered red. Deia's rocking chair dips unevenly on its side, stray wood splintering through the hem.

At her feet lies the torn carcass of a black beast.

NeedleTeeth.

Its head is detached, tossed to the side of its mangled body.

She continues through the home, sighing with relief as she spots Deia. She sits at her messy table, dough and flour strewn about in their usual manner, seemingly untouched. Alara starts towards her, her stomach sinking further. "Deia?" she whispers.

She doesn't respond. Alara circles slowly, one foot in front of the other. She takes her time as she draws near. Her heart pounds in her chest with each step. She extends a shaky hand, resting it on Deia's shoulder. She doesn't respond to her touch. She loosens her grip and Deia slumps forward, tumbling out of her chair.

Alara's breathing stops. Deia lays motionless on the floor. Her skin is tight with the appearance of old leather, sunken in at the cheek bones. Her eyes are missing, replaced with a thick, black ooze. Her complexion, usually vibrant and glowing, is now a sick grey hue.

Alara reaches for her, pulling her into her embrace. She feels shrivelled and rough under her touch. Alara squeezes her tightly, sobbing through the nightmare. Her mind races to memories they have shared over the years, her influence always a strong force leading her forward. Deia had always been there for Alara and Alec, for the entire village really. She had always given Alara fresh stew and bread, comfort and love. Gifting her the hope she needed to continue in her duties. Alara pulls her closer, stifling a scream into her stiffened shoulder.

She cries out with an unparalleled urgency as the gravity of what has happened here slams into her. "Alec!" she shouts, resting Deia on the floor and tearing from the room.

Silence.

Alara hurls herself towards the back of the cottage, into the room Deia's own children once claimed. The room Alec has been occupying.

The room is peaceful. Frozen in time. It's decorated with wooden toys, scratched and well-loved. A rocking horse rests in the corner, collecting dust. Two of the beds are neatly folded. The third has been recently slept in, the blankets dishevelled, tangled amongst several scraps of loose parchment. Alara approaches them, grabbing one of the papers in her hands. She raises it into her vision and quickly drops it from her grasp. She shifts back to the heap of drawings on the bed, each one an echo of the last. Messy charcoal streaks smudge across the parchment, creasing the pages. A thick black shadow mocks her. Familiar antlers jut from the figure's skull.

    Alara clutches at her chest, her heart throbbing beneath her palm. She drops to the floor, bowing her head beneath the bed. "Alec!" she screams, her voice raw and desperate. She crawls forward, clawing through paper and clothing, searching for the piece of her she has lost. Alec is nowhere to be seen. The smell of him lingers in the room, taunting her through her anguish, leading her into another dead end. The drawings flurry around her, twisting through the air.

    One is different from the others. It catches Alara, luring her into it. The same silhouette greets her but it is smaller, not alone. Its hands reach out to the sides, each one grasping another soul. Alara recognizes herself, her dagger clutched firmly in her palm. On the other side, Alec, his curly hair wild and unmistakable.

    The Blood is Mine.

The thought thunders through her mind, the voice behind it still unknown.

"Alara!" Bram's voice rings through the horror. She folds the parchment and packs it into her pocket. He calls again.

Alara turns towards the sound, reluctant to leave but shuffles on. As she heads back to the village, her gaze sticks on a smear of red, coating the back door's frame. She hesitates a moment before diverting her path. The stain blooms larger as she approaches, growing fingers beyond a slender palm. Alara clenches her jaw tightly, the room blurring behind unshed tears. She reaches her hand out, placing it gently over Alec's bloodied handprint.

Outside the sky still burns, threatening the earth below. She follows the sound of Bram's desperate calls, stepping over the remains of Ravenforge.

Alara finds him just a foot away from the overgrown trail. He is crouched low, hunched over something with his ear to the ground. She moves to his side and stifles a gasp attempting to escape her lips.

"So many eyes... So many teeth..." Bram staggers back as Alara approaches. She gets low, meeting Serlida's severed head, her rumoured immortality ringing true, tethering her soul to the ruined village, as she continues to whisper. Her brows are drawn in terror. "The mark has been made. The dead demand their funeral."

"Auntie?" Alara gasps, despair flooding over the name. Alara reaches out to her, fingers just an inch from Serilda's face and freezes. Serilda's skin, usually white as paper, now appears almost translucent with dark blue veins sprouting out sporadically in all directions. The base of her neck is a jagged ruin. Flesh dangles around muscle and vertebrae. A hooked claw protrudes from the torn skin by her throat, embedded deep below the jawline, curving out through the other side. The ground is damp with dew, not blood.

Serilda blinks in a flurry, meeting Alara's eyes. Her breath quickens as her sense returns. "Alara... my girl. Where... Where did I go?" Her eyes dart back and forth, trying to make sense of the state she is in. "I can't feel anything."

Alara looks around for Serilda's body but it is nowhere in sight. She scrambles through the dirt, inching closer. She lowers her face to Serilda's and places her hands on her cheeks. "It's okay, Auntie," she sobs. "It's going to be okay."

Serilda's eyes steady, her panic melting away. She smiles. "Do you hear that?" she whispers. "The baby's awake." Serilda raises her voice, it carries through the silence sharply. "Mommy is coming, my boy."

Alara blinks at her, swallowing back her tears. She stands, lifting her gaze to the roads and trails of Ravenforge. They are littered with the remnants of her people. Limbs swallowed by ash and flies.

Bodies scatter the road, heaped amongst themselves and slumped in doorways. Their faces are torn and bloodied, their torsos bruised and scarred. Some are friends, family. Others are shredded beyond recognition, their faces ripped violently away. Several corpses appear drained and shrivelled, their eyes caved in, leaking black. The same way she had found Deia.

Oh Gods, Deia.
Alec.
Auryn.
Serilda.

Her every purpose, reduced to slaughter. To mud. To blood. To nothing.

The dead surround her in every direction. Blood paints the cobblestone, drying under the strange, bleeding sky.

"The baby. Do you hear the baby?" Serilda's face lights up and her eyes flicker back and forth. "I hear him. My baby."

Alara staggers away from Serilda's pleading voice, every step she takes pulling her into a deeper haze. Her chest is tight, each breath heavy with smoke and iron.

The trees stand just beyond the last row of shattered cottages. She moves to the forest's edge, forcing back the spinning inside her head. She reaches out, catching herself on a low branch. It's soft and warm. Its edges are too smooth to belong to bark. She looks down at her hands.

A foot.

The colour is leached a sickly grey. Her fingers recoil. She pulls away involuntarily. Alara steps back, her eyes climbing the length of the leg, past the withered muscle, to the torso slumped and sunken into the skeleton.

Councilman Thomas stares down at her. Nails stick out from his palms, his limbs splayed and pinned with iron spikes. His face appears inverted, his skin dry and dark. His eyes have been plucked from their sockets. Small wooden swords meant for child's play are lodged in their place.

Alara's head spins as she looks to her right. Councilwoman Elowen is hanging at his side, her body displayed in the exact manner of Thomas. Her hood, normally pulled low over her face, is pushed back, giving Alara the perfect view of her tarnished state.

She forces her eyes further to the next tree. Elder Tilda, who has never once bowed to anyone, is suspended from the trunk. Her spine is stiff from the metal rod that has been weaved through her, forcing her at a bend. Her head is low in unwilling surrender. Her arms have been yanked to the sides of the bark and ran through with rusted nails.

Alara stares at the bodies on display.

This is no work of the NeedleTeeth.

The mindless beasts lack the intellect to create such a statement.

Brams steps up beside Alara. She wavers on her feet and he catches her by the arm, slumping her onto his shoulder. Her eyes flicker between the council members, their fate too horrible for her to break her gaze.

"Everyone is dead," Bram states, his voice thundering through Alara's numbness. She pushes off of him, stepping backwards, scanning the ruined village surrounding them. "What do we—"

Alara breaks off in a jog. She races towards the forest, stumbling over limbs as she navigates the path. She throws herself into the sprint, as though her feet can escape the reality behind her. Bram calls out but she is unable to slow down. She bursts through the torn remnants of the fence—its failure to protect the village more catastrophic than ever. Her broken sigils blur as she runs past, the iron shavings scattered like confetti.

She falls to the forest floor in utter defeat. Alara's stomach tightens as her mouth begins to salivate. She lurches into the dirt, expelling the horror that has befallen Ravenforge.

When there is nothing left, she wipes at her mouth. She screams at the trees, daring them to take her too. She screams until her ribs feel like they may snap. She screams until her throat goes raw and she tastes iron, coughing up the blood in her throat. She pounds the earth with her fists, before unsheathing her dagger. She drives it into the dirt, again and again. She stabs at it as though she can dig a hole large enough to bury her people.

Her grip slips on the handle. The palm of her hand slides down the steel, slicing it wide open. She wails and starts digging frantically with her bare hands, feeling the dirt under her fingernails. Her knuckles scrape raw, the soil filling the open wounds. Her arms tremble until they give out altogether. Alara falls forward, pressing her forehead into the bloodied soil.

She blinks up at the burning sky and glances around through the stillness of the trees. Away from Ravenforge, the air is peaceful and forgiving. Alara could allow herself to stay here. She sighs heavily, closing her eyes in surrender.

A stick cracks. Alara whips her eyes open to meet Jax's frozen stare. He is breathing fast. He wears no smirk. His lips look different, darker. She squints at them before noticing they've been stained. Blood trickles delicately down his jaw. In his hand he clutches a braided bracelet, the bronze charm glaring down at Alara.

Alec's bracelet.

Alara springs back up to her feet, snatching her dagger from the forest floor in one swift movement. Jax's nostrils flare, his focus fixed on her injured hand. His skin shivers, the veins beneath them pulsing green against the surface. They crystalize as they push outwards, scaled cracks severing through his once porcelain complexion. The corners of his mouth split open, his jaw dislocating and tearing away from him.

    Alara steadies herself, poising her dagger between them, her hands shaky and loose. Jax snarls and saliva drips through the sharp points of his teeth, gnashed together in sporadic form. She lunges at him.

    Jax sprints forward, his eyes yellow with thin black slits extending, cold and unblinking, the world around them sharpening to a single, predatory focus.

    He collides into Alara, knocking their bodies to the ground. She winces, struggling to free herself from his weight forcing down on her. She drives her dagger into his side, twisting it before pulling it out and stabbing it between his ribs, burying it deep in his flesh, the hilt preventing the steel from reaching his heart. A low, animalistic growl forms in his throat as his fingers wrap around the brass chain she wears in mourning. He rips it from her, the clasp breaking with the motion. He holds it in his hand, mindlessly twisting it around Alec's bracelet, his eyes fixed on her as she writhes beneath him. Jax distends his jaw, pressing his mouth to her throat, pinning her arms to the forest floor. His breath is warm and humid on her skin as his front teeth poke against her, blood pooling beneath them.

    Alara shrieks and everything goes black—except his eyes, serpentine and famished.

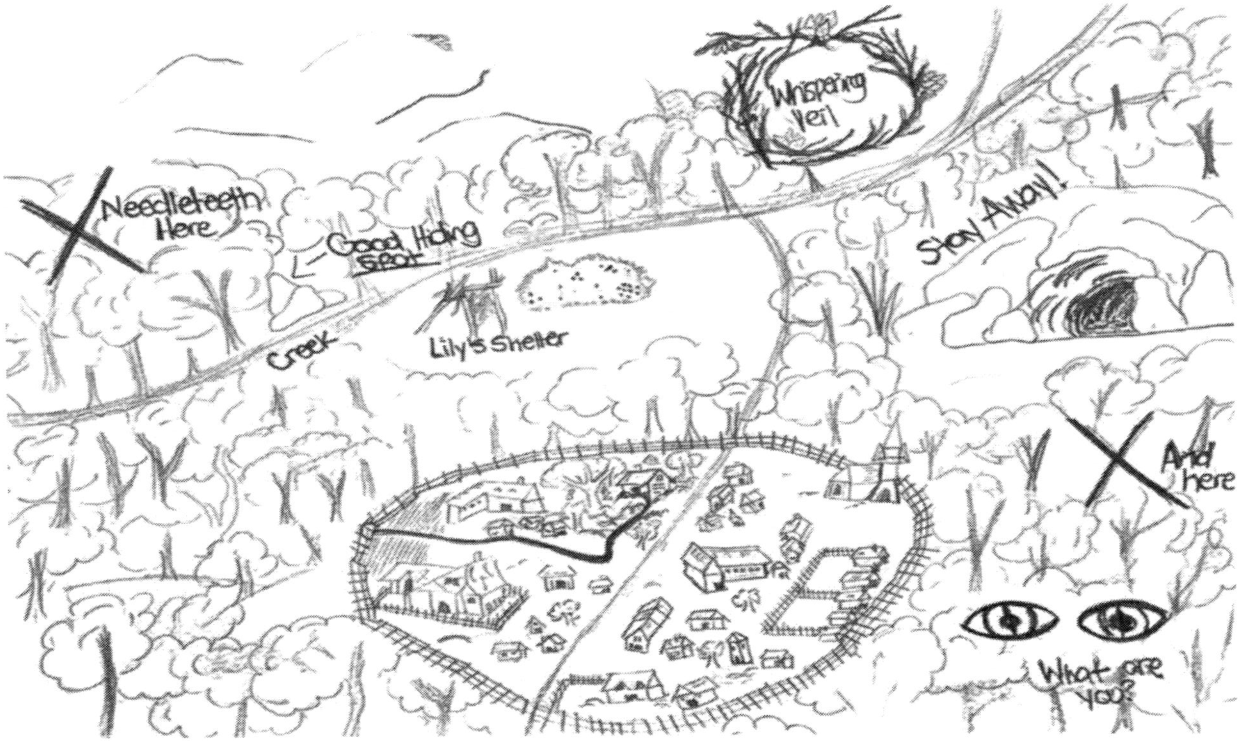
Needleteeth Here
Good Hiding Spot
Creek
Lily's Shelter
Whispering Veil
Stay Away!
And here
What are you?

Click click click

NeedleTeeth

If you see one more are coming

Hide

good to talk to

Scabs

safe

Do not like sweets

Can look like anyone

The Swarm

Do NOT Follow

Stay with us

We were waiting for breakfast when the screaming started. They came so ~~fast~~. I ran but we got split up. When I looked back she was gone and Ravenforge was on fire. I can still smell the blood. I think one of them is ~~following~~ me.

Where do I go now?

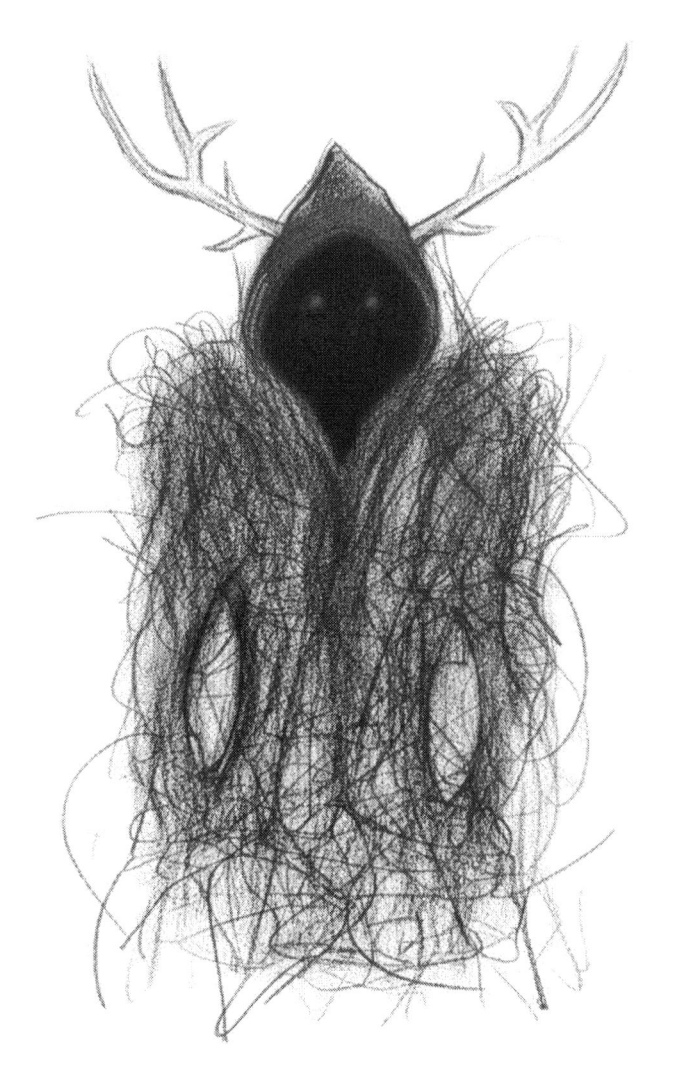

The blood is mine

Manufactured by Amazon.ca
Bolton, ON

50457359R00185